The Night Prowler

A DI Erica Swift Thriller, Volume 12

M K Farrar

Published by Warwick House Press, 2023.

The Night Prowler
A DI Erica Swift Thriller
Book Twelve
Copyright © 2023 M K Farrar
Edited by Emmy Ellis
Cover Design by Marissa Farrar
Published by Warwick House Press

License Notes

All rights reserved. No portion of this book may be reproduced, copied, distributed or adapted in any way, with the exception of certain activities permitted by applicable copyright laws, such as brief quotations in the context of a review or academic work. For permission to publish, distribute or otherwise reproduce this work, please contact the author at mk@mkfarrar.com.

Publisher's Note

This is a work of fiction. Names, characters, places, and incidents are either the products of the author's imagination or are used fictitiously, and any resemblance to actual persons, living or dead, business establishments, events, or locales is entirely coincidental.

Chapter One

A piercingly bright light pressed against her closed eyelids, demanding attention.

Tabitha Moots wanted to ignore it. She fought to remain wrapped in the dark folds of sleep, trying to sink deeper, but it was impossible.

Bright light. Dark room. Middle of the night when she should be sleeping.

Something wasn't right.

Suddenly, with the intensity of the light in front of the thin veils of her eyelids increasing, came the absolute certainty that someone was standing over her.

Tabitha gasped, her eyes springing open, only for her to shut them again as the light pierced her retinas with a surprisingly painful stabbing, blinding her. She twisted her face away, trying to avoid the beam, and half sat at the same time.

Except she didn't manage to get upright, as someone forced her back down to the bed.

A cry of shock and fear tried to escape her lips, but it was stifled by a gloved hand clamping over her mouth.

Understanding about what was happening sank in, but the knowledge brought her no peace. A man loomed over her side of the bed. He'd been shining a torch directly in her eyes to wake her, and now his hand was clamped over her lips to prevent her from crying out for help. Who the hell was he? What did he want? Nothing good, she was sure of that.

A male voice came from beside her in the bed. "What the fuck?"

Somehow, in the horror she'd woken to, she'd forgotten all about her husband. He was awake now, sitting up, staring at the scene illuminated right next to him.

Tabitha didn't know if she should be relieved Jordon was awake or if she should be frightened for him. She was a bit of both. She waited for him to launch himself across the bed, to save her from the man whose hand still covered her mouth. They'd only been married six months—though they'd been together for two years now—and their love was still very much in the honeymoon phase. She'd always believed they'd grow comfortable and old together, but, for the first time, she wondered if that would happen.

Maybe they'd both die first?

Jordon stuttered with shock. "Wh-who the hell are you?"

The man had a white hood pulled up and drawn tightly around his face.

"Try something stupid and I'll kill her without hesitation." He spoke in a low voice, almost a growl, making it hard for her to pick up on any accent.

It was then Tabitha saw the knife. It was large and sharp—the kind she had in the kitchen that she'd use on a Sunday to carve the roast chicken. If this man plunged the blade into her stomach, puncturing internal organs, slashing at her guts, she wouldn't survive. Was she going to survive this anyway? What did he want from them?

She lay frozen beneath the gloved hand. Jordon wasn't doing anything to save her, but then neither was she. She'd always imagined that she'd fight back if she was attacked, that she'd claw and spit and do whatever it took to get free, but now she was like a statue.

Why was no one helping her?

Something else occurred to her. Where the fuck was Duke? The German Shephard crossbreed should be barking the place down at an intruder.

People probably thought they shouldn't keep a dog the size of Duke in a ground-floor flat, but they had a private garden—albeit a tiny one—and it wasn't like everyone in London lived in mansions. Most people of their age didn't even own a place yet and probably never would. She'd always wanted a dog and didn't like small yappy ones so much.

A thought almost worse than that of her own death went through her: had the man hurt their dog? She pictured Duke stabbed and bloodied on the kitchen floor and wanted to cry.

Duke had made her feel safe, but now he was most likely dead, and she was going to end up the same way, too. She'd kill this bastard if he'd hurt her dog.

"Get up," the stranger commanded Jordon. "You stay on the bed, bitch. I'll be back for you in a minute."

"What are you going to do with us?" Jordon managed to say, his voice too high-pitched.

"I'm going to have a little fun. That's what." He snapped his head to one side, as though he'd heard something. "I'll take my time if I want to."

She got the impression he was talking to someone else. Was another person here? Did this sick fuck have an accomplice? Maybe someone who was keeping an eye out in case they were disturbed?

A flare of hope sparked to life inside her. They were in a flat in East London, with neighbours on all sides. Someone might have seen something or heard the disturbance. They could have already called the police, and they were on their way.

Jordon got off the bed.

The man gestured with the knife. "Go into the kitchen."

Tabitha sat up. "No, please," she begged, not wanting to be separated from her husband.

"You stay right where you are. If you move a muscle, I'll cut his fucking throat, do you understand me?"

"Oh God, please don't do this."

"Keep quiet," he said, "or else I'll start cutting pieces off your boyfriend."

He's my husband, she wanted to say, but it didn't matter.

"I'll be back for you."

Tabitha understood what he meant by that.

She'd always felt so blessed. Things in her life had generally gone smoothly. She'd had a good upbringing, with parents who were still together. She'd gone to a decent school, and passed her exams, and then gone on to university and graduated with a first-class degree. Of course there had been bumps in the road, heartbreak and illness, and a few financial worries, but then she'd met Jordon and her world had turned into a fairy tale. They made the perfect couple—everyone said so. They were going to have a wonderful life together and make beautiful babies. Now all of that was over. Even if they did survive this, everything would be changed. She wouldn't be perfect anymore. She'd be sullied, ruined, dirtied.

She clamped her lips shut and remained on the bed, trying to figure out what she should do next. He pushed Jordon out of the bedroom using the hilt of the knife. She watched the figures of the two men leave.

Should she scream? Or try for the window to escape? Where was her phone? If she got her hands on it, then she could call the police herself. She glanced around, but her mobile was nowhere to be seen. Had the man removed the phones before he'd woken them?

If she tried to run or made a noise, would he stab Jordon?

Tabitha was frozen in her indecision.

As long as they both survived, they'd figure out a way to get through this.

She said it as a mantra in her head. *Please let us live. Please let us live. Please let us live.*

A whining came from outside, and her heart lifted. Duke wasn't dead. The bastard had simply put him in the garden, maybe lured him out with a piece of meat or something.

Duke scratched at the back door, still wanting to be let in. Maybe he'd start barking and that would alert the neighbours to something being wrong? It seemed so stupid that they had a guard dog, but he'd been too good-natured to actually do anything about an intruder coming into their home. He'd probably allowed the son of a bitch to scratch him on the head and give him a treat.

The man's voice came from the kitchen.

"Get on your hands and knees," he told Jordon.

"Just do it," Tabitha cried and then clamped her hand over her mouth, remembering she was supposed to stay quiet.

Neither of them were wearing much—Jordon in only his grey Calvin Klein boxer shorts that had seen better days, and her in a camisole and her knickers. At least she wasn't naked, but she didn't know how long that would last.

They just needed to live. Whatever else happened, they would deal with it later.

The man's voice came again. "You, if you drop that, I'll hear it, and I'll know you moved. If that happens, I'll kill her. Got it?"

Followed by Jordon's voice. "No, please, don't do this."

The man laughed. "I'm going to enjoy this, and I'll make sure you hear every moment of it."

Tabitha experienced a surge of anger towards her husband. Why wasn't he doing something? Even if it was risky, didn't he love her enough to try? He was going to kneel in their kitchen, sobbing, while this monster raped her, probably repeatedly.

Then she realised he was doing nothing because he loved her too much. It wasn't his life he was frightened for, it was hers. He didn't want to be the reason this fucker kept his promise and killed her. Was that the same reason she hadn't screamed or tried to run? She was too scared this piece of shit would stab him.

"Don't drop that glass," the man said.

Footsteps sounded, and the man reappeared in the bedroom.

Her shoulders shook, and she covered her face with her hands. "No, please. Don't hurt us."

"Stop it," the man growled, his head snapping around once more. "I told you I would."

She searched the darkness for someone else. Was another person here?

"Please, help us," she cried, just in case there was and she could appeal to their better nature. "Don't let us die."

"Shut the fuck up."

The man swung his arm, and for a second, she thought he was going to stab her. But it was the hilt of the knife he brought down, and it connected with the side of her face, right between her eye and her cheekbone, sending her flying off the bed and crashing to the floor.

The pain was blinding. The room spun, and the darkness seemed to thicken and intensify. Her vision tunnelled. Was she going to lose consciousness? If she did, she doubted she would ever wake again.

He grabbed her by the arm and hauled her back onto the bed. "This is where I need you."

Did she know this man? A spark of recognition lit inside her. Had she met him before?

Tabitha let out a whimper. "Please…"

"You bitch. You dirty, filthy, disgusting whore. You're only good for one thing."

How had this man got into the flat? They always made sure the doors and windows were locked before they went to bed. It was part of their bedtime routine, and nothing had been any different last night. They were aware that people tried their luck around here, especially on ground-floor properties, but she'd been locking their doors against the thought of someone sneaking in to steal their phones or iPads, not this.

He climbed onto the bed with her and tore off her camisole. "If you scream, I'll stab him to death."

She clamped her mouth shut, trying to stay quiet, even while his hand pushed between her thighs.

Was that a second voice she heard over the sounds of her sobs? Over her heartbeat rushing through her ears? She was hearing things, her distraught mind playing tricks on her.

"Help," she sobbed. "Please, help us."

The man lifted the knife. "What did I say about keeping quiet?"

Chapter Two

It was shortly after nine a.m., and this average street in Bow, East London, had become the setting for something out of a horror film.

DI Erica Swift climbed out of her vehicle and took a moment to assess the surrounding area. Houses opposite the crime scene looked directly into the front windows of the property. The road had been blocked at both ends by uniformed police and response vehicles, but that didn't stop nosy neighbours craning their necks to get a better view.

Had one of them been a witness to this horrific crime? All she'd been told so far was that a young couple had been found murdered in their home. The attending police officers had been forced to break in—both the front and back door locked.

Had the couple done this to each other? It was unlikely, but the locked doors was strange.

Before she had the chance to approach the crime scene, a second car pulled up behind her. She already knew who it was without even turning to see. She'd left her sergeant less than an hour earlier, at home, but they couldn't arrive together this early in the morning. While she suspected people at the office knew something was going on between the two of them, no one had confronted them directly—or at least confronted her. She was the one who'd be in trouble for not declaring their relationship to their DCI yet.

There was no denying that her being a senior officer to Shawn was a power imbalance and had the potential for creating conflict within the team. She'd hate for the rest of her team to think she wasn't being impartial when it came to him. While she hoped they knew her well enough to understand that she would be, the relationship would be something that could be used against her.

If that happened, the only option would be for one of them to move departments.

As the weeks and months had gone by, they'd created a new family unit around her daughter. Before, she hadn't realised how much laughter was missing from her home. It wasn't that she and Poppy hadn't laughed together—they had—but it was different when you heard laughter coming from another room, laughter from two people you loved most in the world. Because she'd known and cared about Shawn for years, it wasn't as though their relationship was like starting from scratch. They'd just kind of picked up from where they'd always been heading.

She wouldn't be making the decision purely for her daughter either. It would be for her, too—having an adult in the house, someone to talk to when Poppy was asleep.

It was the mundane things she'd discovered she'd missed the most. Having someone else say 'I can do that' and take it off her plate—like remembering to take the bins out on the right day, or throw her a clean towel when she'd forgotten to take one into the bathroom for her shower, or pick up some milk because he'd noticed they were running low—was a simple comfort. Now she'd allowed herself to be open to it, she'd discovered she couldn't bear the thought of giving it up again.

In work, they kept a purely professional relationship. They both understood how important it was.

Shawn greeted her, and they both checked in with the uniformed officer at the outer cordon and ducked beneath.

A stout woman in her forties exited the building, talking to someone. She spotted Erica and Shawn, recognised them for who they were, and headed over.

"Detectives, thanks for coming. I'm Sergeant Carys Jones."

Erica detected a faint Welsh accent. She introduced them both then asked, "What do you know so far?"

Sergeant Jones grimaced. "Young couple, murdered in their home. Thirty-one-year-old Tabitha Moots, and thirty-three-year-old Jordon Moots. They'd only been married six months."

"You're sure it's murder?" Erica asked.

The sergeant sucked air in over her teeth. "Well, the doors were all locked when we arrived, but, when you see the state of the victims, you'll understand why the theory they did this to themselves is unlikely."

Shawn glanced over at the house. "Who discovered the bodies?"

"The responding officers. We got a call from the neighbours, concerned because the couple's dog—a German Shephard cross—was out in the garden, barking all night. They said it was extremely unusual for the animal to be left out and thought something might have happened."

It was interesting that the couple had a dog, and a big one at that. Why hadn't the dog alerted them to the intruder? Most intruders avoided places with dogs. It was simply easier to break into a property without one.

"The neighbours didn't go to investigate themselves?" Erica checked.

"No. They were frightened the dog would try to attack them, though he seems soft as anything to me. These breeds get a bad rap when half the time it's the owners who are the problem, not the animal."

Shawn frowned. "Does the dog seem soft enough that it would let someone break into the flat and do this?"

Sergeant Jones shrugged. "Hard to say, really. If the killer touched him, we might be able to get evidence from him. You never know."

"Did the neighbours see or hear anything else?" Shawn asked.

"The ones who reported the dog barking didn't, but we're still asking around."

Erica took in the street. It was built up, with plenty of people around. The crime might have happened during the night, but everyone knew that London didn't really sleep. Someone must have seen or heard something.

"Check for doorbell video cameras as well," Erica suggested, "or other CCTV from the neighbourhood."

"My officers are already onto it," Jones said.

Shawn peered over her shoulder at the house. "Do we know how the killer got in yet?"

"Not yet. Back door was locked, though it must have been unlocked at some point in order to put the dog out. Front door locks automatically. No sign of forced entry anywhere. No windows broken or anything like that."

Erica glanced over at Shawn. "Strange. Maybe he had a key?"

"Maybe," he agreed. "Someone they knew then?"

Erica turned her attention back to Sergeant Jones. "What about the victims? Any dealings with the police?"

Jones pursed her lips. "No, none whatsoever. Clean as a whistle. No indication that they've had any problems with anyone recently."

"Until now," Shawn added.

The sergeant grimaced. "Until now. There's something else, something you need to see."

"What is it?" Erica asked.

"You really need to see for yourself."

They pulled on protective outerwear before ducking under the inner cordon and entering the house. It was a normal, tidy home for a reasonably well-off childless couple. A few pieces of art on the walls, photographs of the previously happy pair in warm, sunny places. Some wedding photographs.

She nodded to the Scenes of Crime Officers, who were similarly dressed as she was, as they moved around the property, taking photographs, marking anything of importance, and collecting samples.

"It's through here," Sergeant Jones said.

She stopped in front of the entrance hall wall.

Erica's heart thudded, and she drew a breath.

Each letter was ten inches tall and written on the wall in blood.

You have to stop him.
I'm not strong enough.

"We don't know whose blood it is yet," Jones said. "We assume it's one of the victims' or maybe a mixture of both."

Shawn arched his brow. "Let's hope the killer was stupid enough to use their own. Unlikely, I know, but it wouldn't be the first time a criminal has done something dumb. Besides, these words indicate to me that perhaps they want to get caught."

"Or they had someone with them who wants to get him caught," Erica said.

Jones glanced between them. "You think there might be two of them?"

Erica nodded. "It's certainly possible. Let's take a look at the victims."

"Of course. The male is on the floor in the kitchen. The female is on the bed in the bedroom. Let's go to the male first, since we're closer."

Sergeant Jones led them into the kitchen.

Erica had seen plenty of blood in her time, but this was a lot, even for her. A pool of it congealed around the man's body. He'd been stabbed multiple times. Splashes of blood were across the kitchen cupboards, worktops, and over the walls.

"There's anger in this killing," she said. "Hatred even. People don't stab others this many times without there being some kind of intense emotion behind it."

"Are there any signs of a burglary?" Shawn asked.

Sergeant Jones pinched her lips. "Not that we've found so far. The couple's iPhones and iPads were still in the flat. We found the female victim's purse, too, which appears to be untouched. Unless they were after something we haven't yet worked out is missing, I'd say this isn't a robbery gone wrong."

"Besides," Erica mused, "who stabs someone this many times in a burglary? If the perp had expected the place to be empty and got taken by surprise, I could understand them stabbing once or twice, lashing out because they were desperate, but this is far worse than that. What about the murder weapon?"

"No sign of it so far. We're still searching."

Erica crouched to study the body of Jordon Moots. She placed her gloved hand to the side of his neck. The skin was already cool to touch. He'd been dead for several hours.

"What's he doing in the middle of the kitchen floor?" she said half to herself. She tried to piece together the time leading up to their deaths. "It doesn't appear as though he was running for help."

Something in the blood caught her eye.

"What's with the glass?" Erica bent and picked up a piece of the bloodied glass in her gloved hand.

She held it towards the light, turning it one way and then the other. She straightened and went to the kitchen cupboards, opening one after the other. She found what appeared to be part of the base of the tumbler. "I think it's one of these that's smashed on the floor around him. They have four of everything, and one of these is missing."

"Maybe Jordon got up in the night, got himself a drink of water from the kitchen, and then was attacked by the assailant," Shawn suggested. "He could have dropped the glass then, and it smashed."

She glanced over at the tap. "Possible, but he didn't have the chance to get the water. There's none on the floor."

Shawn shrugged. "So he was attacked before he reached the tap."

Erica turned to Sergeant Jones. "Let's take a look at the female victim."

Together, they went into the bedroom.

The woman lay on her back on the bed, naked. She'd also been stabbed multiple times. The blood had soaked into the mattress around her.

"We suspect sexual assault on the woman," Jones said. "A torn camisole and underwear that we believe belong to her are on the floor beside the bed."

A small yellow numbered placard had been placed next to the bloodied bundle of clothing.

"Jesus," Shawn said, shaking his head. "These poor people."

Erica felt the same way. What a terrible ending to two innocent lives.

Jones continued, "From the amount of blood surrounding them, I'd say they were killed in the same spots their bodies were found. The bodies weren't moved or staged at all."

Erica looked between the two rooms, trying to piece together what had happened in the moments leading up to their deaths.

"Who was killed first? Tabitha or Jordon?"

"Most likely they killed Jordon first and then dragged Tabitha into the bedroom, raped her, and murdered her," Shawn said.

"But what was Tabitha doing while they killed Jordon? We'll know the exact number of times he was stabbed once the postmortem has been carried out, but from an initial observation, it must be around ten times. It takes time to plunge a knife into someone, pull it out again, and then repeat over and over. Tabitha could have made a run for it while it was happening." Erica leaned in over the body, searching for any signs that she might have been tied up. "There are no obvious ligature marks."

"She might have been locked in somewhere," Shawn said. "Or maybe there *was* more than one attacker?"

"Or she just froze? People react in lots of different ways when they're in mortal danger. Some lose it and scream and fight, while others retreat into themselves."

Shawn took several steps around the bed. "Or the killer or killers told them to stay put. Cooperation in the hope of survival can be a powerful motivator."

Erica glanced back down at the body. "With any luck, we'll get some DNA from the bodies, especially Tabitha's. There's a possibility the perp didn't use protection and we can get a sample of semen from her body and match it with someone on our system."

Already, she was thinking about any known sex offenders from around the area. No one in particular came to mind. Had any rapists been released from prison back into the community recently? Years of being behind bars might have built up their frustration to the point that once they were freed, this was the result.

"Have their next of kin been informed?" Erica asked Jones.

"Not yet. I have uniformed officers on their way to both Tabitha's and Jordon's parents now."

She couldn't imagine receiving the news that her son or daughter had been brutally murdered in their own home overnight.

When you went into your home and locked your door behind you, you assumed you were safe.

This couple couldn't have been any more wrong.

Chapter Three

Liam stood over the bathtub, the rumble of water filling the porcelain like a waterfall, echoing around the room. Cold water was important. His father had told him that. Hot water fixed the blood into the material.

He picked up the bottle from the floor beside the tub. It had a childproof cap, but it wasn't as though he was a small child anymore. He was strong enough to push the cap down and turn it, opening the bottle. There was a certain quantity he was supposed to use, but he couldn't be bothered to measure it out. Instead, he tipped the bottle upside down and squeezed the hydrogen peroxide into the water.

Beside him was the black bin liner full of the bloodied clothes, and another item, too. He waited until the bath was full, and then he grabbed the bag and emptied the clothes out, but made sure to leave the other item inside.

His father's clothes dropped into the water. Air trapped inside the legs and sleeves caused them to swell and bubble, acting like a float above the water. Liam stared at them for a moment and then used a metal potato masher to plunge the clothes in and out of the water.

The sight of the blood dispersing into the water didn't affect him the way it might some. He wasn't squeamish. Besides, his father had explained to him what needed to happen, and he understood that.

He had to do a good job, or his dad would be angry, and Liam was always frightened of his father's anger. He'd never hit

Liam, but his words were worse than violence. Nothing was worse than being told that he had disappointed his dad.

The chemicals stung his eyes, and he blinked fast.

The hydrogen peroxide might take the colour out of the items, too, turning the black to a dirty, rust-like shade, but that didn't matter. It wasn't illegal to have badly washed-out clothes, but it would cause problems if the blood was detected on them.

It was no good throwing the items away. Thrown away items could be found, and then they could be used as evidence.

His father had done his best to keep blood off the clothing, but even the tiniest speck could be enough to get him caught.

The water swirled around the material, mesmerising him.

He knew what the blood meant. He wasn't stupid. Dad had hurt someone—hurt them badly.

Liam understood why. His dad was at war, and sometimes being at war meant people got hurt. He was going to follow in Dad's footsteps, just as soon as he was old enough. It was what he'd been raised to do, but sometimes, he dared to dream of living a different kind of life. In his books, he read stories of sailors who crossed oceans and battled wild creatures or pilots who flew planes to whole other countries. Liam had never even been on a plane. He didn't go to school and rarely left the house, except for at nighttime when his father said it was safe. He couldn't imagine what it would be like to be so high in the sky that he could look down on the earth and see everyone as tiny little dots. It must be thrilling.

He never let Dad know that he harboured such ideas. He could just picture the disappointment in his father's eyes, the shake of his head, the tutting of his tongue against the roof of his mouth. That kind of life was a fantasy. This was his real one, and he couldn't escape it.

Liam gave the clothes enough time to soak, and then he pulled out the plug and let the dirty water run down the drain. When the bath was empty—aside from the sodden clothes—he put the plug back in and refilled the tub with clean water. He'd need to do this several times to make sure the clothes were really clean.

Then he had the black bag still containing the other item to deal with.

He grinned down at it. The bag meant he'd be allowed to go into the garden. It would be dark, but Liam didn't mind. It was a treat to sit around the small metal fire pit, watching the flickering flames and warming his hands.

Liam didn't go out in the daylight. If he did that, the neighbours would see him, and that would be bad. They would ask questions and make things difficult for Dad.

No, more than difficult. His father had already explained how they could come and take Liam away.

Busybodies. That's what his father called them. Stupid women who didn't know how to keep their noses out of other people's business. They had nothing better going on, so they had to interfere in the lives of others.

His father said that these women saw them as a threat because they refused to become the subservient males that women wanted them to be. They'd cut their cock and balls off, if they could, and have them running around, doing their bidding.

Liam didn't want someone cutting off his cock and balls. It was only recently that he'd really figured out what they were for.

His father said that using women for sex was fine but that he shouldn't get his hopes up. Women didn't want men like them. They wanted men who were over six feet tall, and who had chiselled jaws, and who earned lots of money. That didn't mean they shouldn't take it, though, even if the women weren't that keen. It was a human right to be able to have sex, and women shouldn't be allowed to keep it from them.

Liam wasn't sure what to make of that, especially since he was old enough to know that he'd been born after his father had had sex with a woman. His mother. Did that mean his mother hadn't wanted to have sex with Dad? That Liam had been born because of that?

It was something he tried not to think about. There were lots of things he tried not to think about. He imagined he had a box in the back of his head where he could put things that seemed to wriggle around in his brain in the dead of night, keeping him awake and making him uncomfortable in a strange kind of way he couldn't really describe.

Whenever he tried to ask his dad about things that bothered him, he quickly got shut down. Dad used words like 'ungrateful' and 'disappointed' and told him that he couldn't possibly understand.

He would one day, though, when he was grown.

Liam wouldn't stay young forever.

Chapter Four

By the time Erica and Shawn returned to the office, it was approaching lunchtime. Erica hadn't found a moment to eat yet. First, she needed to brief her team.

In the briefing room, she pieced together everything they'd learned so far about the incident. She pinned maps of the area and photos of the crime scene to the board. She included pictures of the victims—how they'd looked before they'd been killed, and then more photographs of the bloodied states they'd been found in. They were almost unrecognisable.

What must be going on in a person's head to stab someone that many times?

She pressed her hands over her face, pushed back her hair, and let out a breath. She'd seen a lot of violent cases in her time, but something about this one had got under her skin. She pictured the killer overcome with rage, almost unaware of what they were doing as they'd brought the knife down over and over. What had the young couple done to make someone murder them with such hatred?

She looked at the photographs of the words that had been written in what they assumed to be the victims' blood.

You have to stop him.
I'm not strong enough.

Erica felt the message had been written for her. It was her job to stop the killer, but from what? Striking again? Was the murderer planning another attack? Or had he done it before?

She analysed the words.

'Him' not 'me'. Was this one person with some kind of dissociative personality who was thinking about 'himself' or another version of himself, in the third person? Or could it be that there was a second person, and they'd taken the opportunity to write the message when the killer was distracted. Why the cryptic message, though? If this second person did want to stop him, why not write the killer's name or even their initials—something that would be of actual use to them?

She wondered if it might be of use to speak to a psychologist or even a forensic handwriting specialist to see if they could give some insight into what the two sentences might mean.

Shawn brought her a coffee—black and sweet, just how she took it.

She had a sip and grimaced. It was bitter and unpleasant, even worse than normal. Maybe the machine needed servicing or something.

"How's your coffee?" she asked Shawn.

"Terrible, same as usual."

"Seems worse than usual to me."

"Don't drink it," he said. "I'll grab you a fresh one from around the corner after the briefing."

"You don't need to run around finding me coffee, Shawn."

He grinned at her. "Maybe I want to."

She pushed her cup to one side. "Well, I definitely can't drink that. It's turning my stomach."

Her team filing into the room distracted her from her lack of caffeine. She nodded her hellos at her constables, Hannah Rudd and Jon Howard. Hannah was currently prepping for the sergeants' exam, and it had put Jon's nose out of joint that his colleague had got there first. Erica didn't want to lose Hannah as a detective constable, but she'd done her time and was more than capable of rising through the ranks to sergeant. Though she didn't want to consider the possibility, if there was a chance that Shawn needed to move from the team in the near future, at least she'd have a sergeant in the form of Hannah who she could trust.

She didn't want to think about that, though.

When everyone was sitting down, Erica began.

"At eight-twenty this morning, we received a call from attending officers at the scene to say two bodies had been discovered at the following address." She paused to tap the location on the map on the board. "They'd been called to the property for a welfare check as the couple's dog had been barking in the garden from the early hours of the morning. According to neighbours, the barking began at around three-thirty a.m., which may indicate the time that the attack started, though we don't know that for sure yet. There's a chance it was earlier, and the dog simply didn't start barking until later. There's no sign of blood on the dog, though forensics have taken swabs from his fur, so we're assuming at this point that he was put into the garden before the attack happened."

"Are we working on the assumption that the killer put the dog into the garden?" Jon asked.

"We simply don't know at this point. Maybe the dog needed to go out during the night, and one of the victims opened the back door to let him out, and that's when the killer got in."

Hannah raised her hand. "Why didn't the dog go for whoever killed them? Isn't it a guarding breed?"

"A German Shephard, yes," Erica agreed, looking at the photograph of the animal that was pinned to the incident board. "Maybe it did, but the killer got inside the house and shut the door first. It's really impossible to know at this stage."

"Could the killer have already been in the flat when they came home?" Hannah suggested.

"Possibly, though you'd think the dog would have let the couple know if there was someone in the flat who shouldn't be there."

Hannah nodded in agreement.

Erica continued. "The two victims have been identified as thirty-one-year-old Tabitha Moots and thirty-three-year-old Jordon Moots. Tabitha worked in Human Resources for a high street chain store, and Jordon worked as a sound engineer for a film production company based in Canning Town. We're assuming time of death was in the early hours. Both victims were cool to the touch when officers arrived, indicating they'd been dead for several hours, though we'll know more after the postmortem. They'd only been married six months, no children. Tabitha was found lying on her back on her bed, with multiple stab wounds on her chest and torso, and there are also signs of sexual assault. Jordon's body was found in the middle of the kitchen floor. He'd been stabbed multiple times as well, but in the back. A glass was smashed on the floor beside him."

"Happened in the struggle, perhaps?" Shawn suggested.

"Yes, most likely. Currently, we haven't located the murder weapon which we believe to be a large single-bladed knife. We have search teams working the property and surrounding area in case the killer disposed of the weapon nearby. So far, it doesn't appear as though any knives are missing from the kitchen, but without knowing exactly what was in the drawers, we can't be certain. Nothing is missing from the knife block, however. We have search teams working the local area for anywhere it might have been dumped."

"The killer could have taken it with him," Jon said.

"Perhaps, but that wouldn't be a smart move on his part. If we found that knife either in his possession or on his property, then it would be a short journey to a lifetime behind bars."

Shawn glanced back at Jon. "Criminals make mistakes all the time."

"And God bless them for that," someone called from the back, which elicited a flurry of laughter, lightening the mood.

For Erica, this didn't seem like a killer who would make a stupid mistake. He'd got in and out of the property without being seen, had dealt with a big dog, and no one had heard anything.

This had been planned.

Whoever was responsible had gone there with the intention of brutally murdering Tabitha and Jordon Moots, and they'd prepared for every step of it.

When everyone had settled back down, she carried on with the briefing. "We were able to retrieve two phones and two iPads, and one laptop from the crime scene. Digital Forensics will work to recover messages. Perhaps someone was already threatening the couple. This definitely has the feel of it being personal. Killing two people by stabbing them this many times—someone wanted to be hands-on. They wanted to be completely immersed in the killing."

Erica cast her gaze over the room, making sure her team was following her. The atmosphere was sombre again, and they seemed to be hanging on her every word.

"Local officers have been to break the news to the victims' families. We're going to need to speak to everyone who knew them. Their families, work colleagues, friends. They were recently married. Had that put someone's nose out of joint? An ex-boyfriend, perhaps?" She drew her team's attention to one of the photographs on the board. "Then we have this to consider." She pointed at the photograph of the writing. "What are everyone's thoughts on this?"

"It reads as though someone else wrote it," Hannah said. "Like there was a bystander or an accomplice. Should we consider there being more than one suspect?"

"It's certainly a possibility," Erica agreed. "Not only do we have the literal writing on the wall, speaking about someone else, but there's also the fact that there were two victims, and yet neither tried to escape or scream for help. Was that because the second person was standing over them with a knife?"

Hannah raised her hand to speak. "If SOCO find footprints in the blood, it might help indicate if there were two people involved."

"Or whoever did this is a complete psychopath," Jon offered, "and has had some kind of dissociative break."

Erica looked at him. "You think he might have written this about himself?"

"It's possible, right?"

She nodded. "Perhaps. At this point, anything is. If you have a theory, then I'll hear it."

"Two people makes more sense as far as keeping the victims quiet," Shawn said.

Erica turned back to the board and the crime scene photographs. "We don't yet know what order the victims were killed in. Was Jordon stabbed first, and then his wife raped and murdered? Or was Jordon forced to listen to what happened to his wife before he was killed? It makes sense that there was a second person. If that's the case, someone to stop Jordon trying to escape while the attacker was raping Tabitha. We should know more once the forensic report comes back. With the amount of blood both the victims lost, the attacker will have carried the blood of his first victim on his hands or clothes over to the person he went to last. That should give us an idea, unless he moved between both victims repetitively during the murderers." She took a breath. "Whoever did this must have also left the flat covered in blood. Unless they washed or changed their clothing. Someone walking down the street like that would have been spotted. Did the killer have a car? Or did they get here on foot?"

"On foot would make it easier for the killer to sneak in and out without being seen or heard," Shawn said.

"But they'd have made an escape faster with a vehicle," Jon countered.

Erica gave each of the detectives their actions. "Hannah, can you liaise with uniform, find out if there are any neighbours we need to speak to? Ask if anyone heard a vehicle pulling up outside the house during the night, or one driven away during the early hours. We need to check all the vehicles parked on the street and the surrounding area, find out if there are any that can't be accounted for."

Hannah scribbled in her notes.

"Jon, can you check past cases, see if there's anything that fits."

The detective constable nodded. "Will do, boss."

She wasn't expecting him to find anything. She was sure she'd remember if another couple had been brutally murdered in their homes like this. These weren't the kind of cases that were easy to forget.

Chapter Five

Tabitha Moots' parents lived not too far away in Lewisham, so Erica and Shawn did the drive over to their address.

Jordon was from Sheffield, and his family still lived there, so it wasn't practical for Erica to speak directly with them. She'd have to leave that to local detectives. She could talk to Tabitha's family, however.

Erica knew she could have given this job to one of her colleagues, but it was important to her that the parents knew she was fully involved in finding their daughter's killer. She wanted to be able to look them in the eye and reassure them of that.

She also wanted to find out if they knew anyone who might have wanted to hurt Tabitha.

Shawn rang the bell, and they waited for the door to be answered. It wouldn't be likely that Tabitha's parents would be out. Who would want to go out in public after getting that kind of news?

She was also aware that while there was no indication that the parents had anything to do with the couple's death, she also needed to rule them out. It would be highly unlikely for them to be the culprits of such a terrible killing, especially with sexual assault involved, but sadly the world was a sick and twisted place, and Erica never wanted to rule anything out until proven otherwise.

A man opened the door, red-eyed and pale-faced.

"Mr Filer?" Erica asked. "I'm sorry to disturb you, but I'm DI Swift, the lead investigator on your daughter and son-in-law's case. This is DS Turner. I wondered if we could ask you and your wife some questions?"

He shook his head. "I'm sorry, Detective, but the doctor gave my wife some sedatives. She was hysterical, understandably. She's sleeping now."

"It's okay, I don't want you to disturb her. When she's feeling better, we will want to speak to her, but not until then."

He sniffed. "Not until she's feeling better? Is that ever going to happen? It's not as though she's picked up a bug, is it, or even that she's got cancer? This isn't something she's ever going to recover from. Neither of us are."

"Let's go inside, Mr Filer," Erica said. She didn't want them to have this conversation on the doorstep. They were lucky there was no press around, but that probably wouldn't last. "I'll make you a cup of tea."

He nodded and shuffled backwards without a word. Shawn led the way, and Erica stepped in after and gently shut the door behind her, mindful of Mrs Filer asleep upstairs.

Shawn guided Mr Filer into the living room to sit down. Erica found the kitchen and busied herself making the tea. Tabitha's father didn't make any attempt to stop her. She put the kettle on and opened and shut cupboards, searching for a mug. The kitchen wasn't very big, so it didn't take her long to get the tea brewing.

She carried it into the living room.

"There you go," she said, setting the mug down in front of him. "I hope it's how you like it."

Mr Filer put his head in his hands, seeming unaware of what she'd just said. "My poor Tabitha. God, how can something like this have happened to her? Her life torn away from her. We loved Jordon, too. He was like a son to us. I just can't believe this has happened. I keep wanting to wake up, thinking I'm in a nightmare, but I can't, can I? This has actually happened, and nothing I can do or say will change anything."

Erica softened her tone. "That's not strictly true, Mr Filer. You might be able to help us find who did this to Tabitha and Jordon."

He swiped at his eyes. "How can I? I don't know who'd do something so terrible."

"There might be things you don't realise you know. Some small detail that might point us to her killer. Sometimes it really is the tiniest of things that means we catch them."

He lifted his face from his hands. "What you're saying is that right now you have no idea who is responsible."

She couldn't lie to him. "Not yet, but it's still very early in the investigation. I have an extremely high success rate when it comes to catching killers, and I don't plan for your daughter's case to be any different."

The muscles in his jaw ticked. "I don't think I've ever felt so angry in my life. No, not even angry. There's no word to describe how I feel. Fury isn't even enough. I swear, if I got my hands on whoever did this to our baby girl, I would tear them limb from limb."

She believed him, too.

He carried on talking, almost as though he'd forgotten they were there. "I hate the thought that he's walking around out there. How can he even look himself in the mirror, knowing what he's done, the lives he's destroyed? What's the point in us now? Why should we bother even carrying on? How will anything in our lives ever be any good again?"

He broke down in great heaving sobs, and Erica's chest tightened, her eyes prickling with unshed tears in the force of this man's grief.

"I realise this is incredibly difficult for you, Mr Filer, but if I could take a moment to ask you some questions, it really could help us track down the person who did this."

He nodded and wiped his eyes. "Yes, of course. I'll answer whatever you need me to. Hell, I'd cut off my own damned leg and hand it to you if I thought that would help."

She wasn't quite sure how to take that comment and moved on. "Is there anyone you can think of who'd want to hurt your daughter?"

The attack had been violent and frenzied. It made Erica think that the culprit was someone who was personally connected to the couple. Could one of them have been having an affair and this was payback? People—and especially women—were normally killed by someone known to them.

"I-I really don't know. The idea that anyone could want to do this to her is just unbearable."

"I understand that, but try to think. Even just a passing comment could be important."

"She hadn't mentioned that anyone had been threatening her. I'd remember something like that." He paused, thinking for a moment. "She hadn't been having a good time at work recently. She'd been finding it hard. She works"—he corrected himself—"*worked* in HR, and they'd been laying off people. There have been a lot of redundancies recently, the company needing to tighten its belt, streamline things. Tabitha was the person who had to deliver the bad news, and people got angry, upset, understandably. But I can't imagine any of them would do something as terrible as this."

"Did she mention any specific names at all? Anyone who was particularly upset?"

He shook his head. "No, she wouldn't have done that. She was very discreet. You'd be better off asking her boss or colleagues."

"Thank you. We'll do that." Erica rested her forearms on her thighs as she leaned in slightly. "What about outside of work? I know she was recently married, but did she have any issues with ex-boyfriends, perhaps?"

"Her ex-boyfriend is a decent bloke. They were together for six years. Honestly, we all thought they were the ones who were going to end up married, but then they split up, and she got together with Jordon pretty quickly after."

Alarm bells rang. "What's the ex-boyfriend's name?

"Reggie. Reggie Mosley."

"Is he local?"

"Yeah, well, London anyway."

"I don't suppose you have a recent phone number or address for him?"

"No, sorry, I don't. He's going to be devastated when he learns about Tabitha. He really loved her. He was broken-hearted when they split up."

Erica exchanged a glance with Shawn. She knew they were thinking the same. Was Reggie Mosley so cut up about it that he'd still be harbouring a grudge two years later? A grudge that ran so deep that he'd break into the couple's home and brutally murder them both?

Tabitha's father seemed to think of something else. "He might even want Duke back."

Erica looked up. "Sorry? What do you mean?"

"He was their dog—Tabitha's and Reggie's. It was decided that Tabitha would take him in the end, because they were more closely bonded, but they got him when they were a couple."

"What kind of relationship did they have? Did she ever mention him getting violent or anything like that?"

"No, I don't think so. They argued, especially near the end, but I don't think he was ever physical with her, at least not that she told me or that I saw signs of. But then people can be good at keeping secrets, can't they?"

She offered him a sympathetic smile. Yes, people could be very good at keeping secrets, sometimes frighteningly so. It was somehow worse when those secrets came out after a person had died. Once they were gone there was no reconciling the new truth. Those left behind would be forced to somehow find peace with it on their own.

Shawn ran through some of the standard questions always asked in these situations: when was the last time Mr Filer had seen his daughter; how had she seemed at the time; was she having any issues with drink or drugs or money? It seemed Tabitha Moots was just a normal, young, professional woman who had nothing to hide.

But someone had wanted her dead, and viciously, too, and Erica didn't believe that Tabitha and her husband had been chosen at random.

When they'd asked all the questions they had for the moment, they thanked Tabitha's father for his time and gave him their condolences once again.

Erica handed him her card. "When your wife feels up to talking to us, please get her to give me a call. Anytime, night or day."

His fingers closed around the card. "I will."

Erica and Shawn left the house and made their way back to the car.

"That was interesting," Shawn said, jangling the car keys in his fingers. "Could Tabitha have fired someone recently? She would have had to deliver a fair amount of bad news to people who might be in desperate situations themselves. The cost-of-living crisis had even hit those who would normally be considered financially comfortable, and perhaps someone had decided Tabitha Moots was at fault."

A job loss could hit people from all levels. It wasn't only about the loss of the place and the colleagues where they spent most of their lives outside of their home. It was also a sense of worth, of contributing, both to their bank accounts and society. Loss of a job might even mean the loss of a home, which could in turn spark a breakdown in relationships and a separation of families.

Erica hated to think that someone would go as far as murdering a couple in their home, but people had been killed for a lot less. There had been a case last month where a man had stabbed a woman at a junction purely out of road rage. He'd accused her of cutting him off at a roundabout and had then followed her until she'd stopped at traffic lights. Then he'd got out of his car and approached hers, dragged her out of the driver's seat, and stabbed her. Luckily, she'd survived, but that was only because of the fast actions of people around them.

"We definitely need to get someone to talk to her boss and colleagues," Erica said. "What about the ex-boyfriend? Think he might be involved?"

Shawn grimaced. "Long-term relationship that ended, only for her to move on right away? Sounds like he might have some resentment there."

She exhaled. "But to wait two years until doing anything? That seems unlikely."

"Something might have triggered him that we don't yet know about. Perhaps he and Tabitha were still in touch—maybe he'd been trying to win her back and she rejected him again?"

"They had a dog together," Erica said, "so the relationship must have been serious."

Shawn pressed his lips into a line as he thought. "Could that be why the dog didn't go for the attacker? Because the dog already knew them and so it went outside with them willingly?"

"That's my thinking, too. We definitely need to talk to Reggie Mosley."

Chapter Six

"Goddamn it."

Sadie Douglas stood beside her car and rifled through her handbag, trying to find her keys. What the hell had she done with them? She'd had them when she'd left the house that morning. She'd locked up after herself, hadn't she, and driven here? Could she have left them in the car?

She cupped her hands to the driver's-side window and peered inside. No sign of them. She tried the handle again, in the hope the car door might have mysteriously unlocked itself while she'd been looking, but it refused to open.

"Shit."

"Is everything okay?"

The male voice came from behind her, making her jump. She'd been so focused on trying to find her keys that she hadn't heard anyone approach. She glanced over her shoulder to find an attractive man in his late thirties or possibly early forties, standing there, his dark eyebrows raised questioningly.

A jolt went through her at the realisation that she was attracted to him. He was definitely older than her, but what did that matter? No, he probably had a wife and kids already. God, even her inner monologue was coming across as desperate. Maybe she was, a little, at least. She'd been lonely recently. It was like all her friends were pairing up and getting married or pregnant, and she was still living alone. Well, not alone. She had her cat, Monty.

A fresh stab of worry went through her. Monty was home alone. How would she get into her house with no keys? She needed to get inside to feed him. He'd be worried if she didn't come home soon.

Stupidly, her eyes filled with tears at the thought of her boy worrying about her. Monty would most likely be perfectly fine, even if his dinner was late. He was probably still asleep on the bed, not even noticing she wasn't home yet.

"Are you okay?" the man asked. "You seem upset."

"Oh. Sorry. I'm just being silly. I've lost my keys, and my cat is home alone."

"Do you have anyone who has a spare? Or do you have one hidden somewhere?"

She offered him a half-smile. "If I told you where I have one hidden, that wouldn't exactly be me being safe."

"No, true. I was only trying to help."

"It's okay, I don't have one hidden somewhere." She let out a sigh. "I guess that's not going to do me much good."

"Could you have left a window open or something? Another way of getting in?" He grinned, revealing a set of straight white teeth, and held up both hands. "Not that I'm suggesting you show me how to break into your house, of course."

He had a good jawline and thick dark hair—the sort she could imagine running her fingers through. She yanked her mind away. She was having a crisis. Now was not the time to be thinking about whether or not this man was dating material. Even so, she found her gaze drifting down to his left hand, searching for a ring. His fingers were reassuringly bare.

Her loneliness stemmed from something far deeper than all her friends getting into relationships. Those who didn't know her history saw a young woman with a near-perfect life, but she'd fought hard to get where she was. Her childhood years, leading into her teens, hadn't been easy. There had been plenty of times where she'd dragged herself through the days, unsure if she'd make it to the next one. Often, she'd believed she was only living for her parents, aware that, like her, they wouldn't survive any more heartbreak.

"My car keys are on that bloody keyring, too," she said. "I can't even drive home."

"Let me give you a lift. I don't mind, honestly."

She shook her head. "I can't put you out like that."

His smile broadened. "Nonsense. I like to think of myself as a hero rescuing a damsel in distress."

Sadie snorted laughter. "I don't normally think of myself as a damsel."

She knew she was attractive. If she was any kind of Barbie, she'd be stereotypical Barbie. She had a nice figure which she maintained by watching what she ate and visiting the gym three times a week. She always kept her hair highlighted to prevent her darker roots from showing, and got her nails done and her eyebrows threaded. But she wasn't a stereotypical 'dumb blonde'. She was thirty-two years old and worked hard as a solicitor in property law. Her good job, combined with an inheritance, had allowed her to buy a home by herself in a halfway decent area—though almost any property was expensive to buy in London these days. The only blight in her adult life had been her so far disastrous relationships. She knew it was partly down to the men she was attracted to—tattooed arseholes from the gym who spent more time looking in the mirror than at her. They always seemed to have some drama or another going on, and she was the one who picked up the pieces for them. When they realised she wasn't too badly off, they hit her up for money as well as sex, and she ended up feeling used.

This attractive man, however, didn't look as though he would need to bother her for money. He appeared to be well enough put together to have his own. Curious, she wondered what kind of car he drove.

No, Sadie, her mother's voice sounded in her head. *You're not going to show a complete stranger where you live and go there with him, alone, and then get him to help you break into your house. What the hell are you thinking?*

Her mum had died when Sadie was twenty-three, from pulmonary heart failure, according to the doctors, though Sadie always believed she'd eventually died from a broken heart, but Sadie still felt like her mum was advising her, if only in her imagination.

But if she didn't take a chance in life, then everything would stay the same, and right now, she wasn't happy. On the outside, she might give the impression she had everything worked out, the career girl who wore the right clothes and carried a designer handbag, but it all felt so shallow.

"Okay, sure," she relented. "A lift would be great."

She could have called an Uber, but then what would she do when she got to her place? She still didn't know how she was going to get inside. She thought of Monty again, alone inside the house. She needed help. And maybe a locksmith.

She said so to her rescuer.

"No point in paying for a locksmith if we can get you inside ourselves. They'll charge you a hundred quid just for coming out."

"You're right," she agreed. "Let's see if I can get inside first."

She'd always considered herself to be security conscious, but maybe she had left the bathroom window open. It always got so damp in there, and the ceiling kept growing a thick black mould, which she'd been religiously wiping away with bleach, but that kept returning. She'd showered first thing, as she always did, so could have left the window open to let the heat and moisture out while she was at work.

"I'm parked over here," the man said.

She didn't comment on the car—not wanting to be one of those kinds of people—but internally, she approved. It was a new silver Volkswagen Passat—not a BMW or an Audi, not a dickhead car, as she thought of them, but a classy vehicle, nonetheless.

She was thinking into this too much. The bloke was just giving her a lift, helping out. It didn't mean he was interested in her in any way.

He opened the car door for her and then took off his jacket and rolled up his shirtsleeves to reveal his forearms. They were attractive forearms, too. Well-muscled, a light spattering of dark hair. She realised she was staring, and her face grew hot. Jesus, she really was desperate to get hooked on a pair of forearms. She was like a man in Victorian times who caught sight of a young woman's ankle.

Sadie gave him her address, and he plugged it into the GPS on his phone and then settled the phone into the holder on the dashboard. He started the engine and pulled out of the car park and into the rush-hour traffic.

"Your wife is going to wonder where you are," she said as he drove.

He glanced over at her, a half-smile turning his lips. "No wife. No girlfriend either."

"Boyfriend?" she said, only partially joking. You never knew these days.

"Nope, not one of them either. What about you?"

"Happily single," she replied and then wanted to kick herself for the 'happily' part. It was a force of habit. She was always having to justify her lack of a husband or kids to people.

"I'm Grant, by the way," he introduced himself.

"Sadie," she replied.

Twenty minutes later, they found a parking space outside her building. They both climbed out. Her flat was on the ground floor, and she gestured to the front door.

"That one's mine."

From the front, there didn't appear to be any windows open. She tried the front door, though she knew it was futile. It locked automatically as soon as it swung shut.

"Okay, how are we going to do this?" Grant asked.

"Let's go around the back," she said. "The bathroom window might be open."

An alleyway led around to the rear of the building. A six-foot wooden gate blocked the way, but it was only held in place with an old, rusted bolt which she yanked open. What had been sold to her as a garden was a ten-foot by ten-foot square of cracked paving slabs, with a few weeds sprouting out of them and a couple of plant pots containing yet more weeds. Any outside space in London was bonus, but Sadie wasn't much of a gardener. Every time she thought to plant something, she promptly forgot about it again, and when she eventually remembered to water it, the plant was normally dead.

Now she found herself embarrassed about the state of the compact space. He didn't seem particularly interested, though.

A furry face peered out at her from the bedroom window.

She sighed. "Oh, Monty."

"Doesn't he have a cat flap?"

"He's an indoor cat," she explained. "There's too much traffic around here for it to be safe for him to go outside. He has a harness, and I bring him out here when the weather is nice, but honestly, I think he'd be happiest lying on my bed."

"Who wouldn't be?" Grant flirted.

Her cheeks burned, and she quickly changed the subject. "Look, the bathroom window is open."

"Think you can fit through?" he asked.

"I'm going to have to try."

The window was only a small one that opened at the top, horizontally. She was glad she kept herself slim or she wouldn't stand a chance. This wasn't going to be her most elegant moment either. She was going to need to wriggle her way through that thing and hope her backside didn't get jammed.

He bent and laced his fingers together to create a kind of miniature hammock.

"What are you doing?" she asked.

"Giving you a boost."

"Oh God." She placed her hand on his shoulder to get her balance. His skin felt hot through the material of his shirt. She wedged her foot into his palm.

He lifted his gaze to meet hers. "Ready?"

"As I'll ever be."

He lifted her, and she reached for the top window, hooking her fingers around the frame. She tried not to think of all the spiders' webs and other bugs that might be crawling around the inside of the frame. Grant supported her weight. She stuck her head through the opening, and then her shoulders. She braced herself, wiggling slightly to get her shoulders through. Her widest point was her hips. What if she got jammed? She'd be so embarrassed. Sadie pictured herself wedged in her bathroom window, the fire brigade called out to try and free her. Them all standing around with a perfect view of her bottom—which Sadie had always thought was too wide—squashed in the window frame.

She hung down over the frame, half in the bathroom now. She was going to have to slither onto the floor and hope she didn't smack her face or break her arm upon landing.

"You doing okay?" he called to her from outside.

"Yeah, I'm almost there."

A furry orange face appeared around the corner of the bathroom door. His yellow eyes widened with alarm, his ears flattening back on his skull.

"Monty! I'm doing this for you. I hope you know that," she panted.

The frame tightened around her rear end, and for a split second, she thought her worst fears were going to come true, but then, like some freakishly huge baby coming into the world via a window instead of a vagina, she slipped into the bathroom. She managed to brace herself with her arms on the floor, though still landed with a thud.

Monty hissed at her and scattered.

"Well, you'd be no good in a crisis," she muttered.

A little bruised, but otherwise none the worse for her ordeal, Sadie picked herself up.

A male voice called from outside, "Everything okay?"

"Yeah. Give me two secs."

She went to the back door, found the key, and opened it. "Ta-da!"

Grant stood there, grinning at her. "Well done."

"Team effort. Thank you so much for your help. How can I repay you?" Suddenly brazen, she added, "How about if I buy you dinner sometime?"

He shook his head, and her heart sank. She'd been sure there was a connection between them, but perhaps she'd been imagining things.

"No need for dinner, but I'd settle for a drink now, if you invite me in?"

Her stomach flipped. So, she hadn't been imagining things.

"I think I have some white wine in the fridge, or maybe a beer."

"Beer sounds good."

"You'd better come in then."

Chapter Seven

Shawn did a background check on Reggie Mosley.

"Nothing alarming comes up," he told Erica. "A caution for drunk and disorderly from a few years ago, but that's all."

"No violence?"

"Not on record anyway. I've got a recent address for him in Wandsworth. Should take us about forty-five minutes to get there."

"Okay, let's do it," she said.

"Can we grab food on the way?" He folded his hands over his stomach. "I'm starving."

It was basically dinnertime now.

She grinned. "You're always starving. It's amazing you're not twenty stone."

"Can't fatten a thoroughbred," he joked.

Erica rolled her eyes and pressed a smile between her lips. Safe to say she was no thoroughbred then. It felt like if she inhaled around a piece of cake these days she put two pounds on each thigh.

She pulled the car into traffic.

"Can you call Jon," she said as she drove, "and ask him to speak to Tabitha's boss and colleagues. See if there's anyone who was particularly upset about being made redundant. Anyone who made threats against her."

"No problem. We need to find out who her friends were, too. Maybe she confided in them about her relationship with either man."

Erica nodded. "Yes, it's definitely worth asking the question, though gently. Anyone close to her is going to be in shock right now. They also might feel as though they want to protect her, even though she's gone. I'm not saying that Tabitha was seeing Reggie, or anyone else, behind Jordon's back, but if she was doing something that people might look down upon her for, a good friend might want to protect her reputation."

"They'd also be potentially protecting a killer."

"Agreed, so that needs to be got across as well."

They were focusing on Tabitha right now, but what if the intended target hadn't been someone from Tabitha's life but from Jordon's? Maybe someone was punishing Jordon for something and made him watch them rape and murder his wife before killing him as well?

She wished she could speak to Jordon's family herself, but she couldn't afford to spend hours on the road. She would have to trust the local detectives for that area that they'd do their job.

They swung by a garage and picked up a couple of sandwiches to eat in the car before continuing on their way. Erica only managed half of her tuna and cucumber sandwich. It didn't taste great—the fish too fishy—and she checked the date on the packet, wondering if it was off. It wasn't, but she still couldn't bring herself to eat the rest.

They went to the address they had on file for Reggie, but he wasn't there.

One of the neighbours saw them knocking. "You after Reggie?"

"Yes, we are," Erica called back.

"He's at his work. He manages the pub around the corner. You can't miss it."

"Thanks, mate," Shawn said.

They left the car parked where it was and reached the pub on foot. It was still early, so the place was practically empty, with only a few men sitting around a small round table. A girl with a nose ring who didn't look to be far out of her teens stood behind the bar, stacking still steaming glasses onto shelves. A football match played on the television positioned on the wall in the corner. The smell of stale beer and fried food hung in the air.

On their side of the bar, a man in his thirties wiped down the counter with a cloth.

"Reggie Mosley?" Erica asked.

The man turned to face them. "Yeah, who's asking?"

Reggie seemed rougher than the type of person she'd have expected Tabitha to be with. He had scruffy dark hair and tattoos up his arms. Was that the reason they'd broken up? He had the 'bad boy' vibe that perhaps a younger Tabitha had been attracted to, but, as she'd grown older, maybe she'd realised didn't make such great husband material.

"Do you have a moment?" She held up her ID. "I'm afraid I have some bad news."

His forehead crumpled, his lips pinching. "Bad news about what? Is my mum okay?"

"Yes, as far as I'm aware. I'm not here about your family."

"Come this way." He led them to a corner booth. "What's this all about then?"

"Where were you last night?" Erica answered the question with one of her own.

"At home. In bed. Like most other people."

"You got anyone who can vouch for you?"

"Yeah, my girlfriend, Lottie." He jerked his head towards the girl behind the bar. "We had a night in, watched a film, had a Chinese takeaway delivered at about nine, and were in bed by midnight."

So that was his girlfriend? There must be a good ten years between them, if not more. But she wasn't there to police relationships. As long as they were both consenting adults, it was none of her business.

"She's your girlfriend?" Erica checked.

"That's right." He bristled. "Got a problem with that?"

"Have you been together long?"

"Three months or so. You going to tell me what this is all about? I've got work to do."

"Do you know Tabitha Moots? She was Tabitha Filer before she got married."

He sat back, his eyes widening with alarm. "Yeah, of course I do. We went out together for years. What's happened? Is she all right?"

"I'm sorry to have to tell you this, Mr Mosley, but Tabitha and her husband were killed last night."

"What do you mean, killed last night? Was there an accident or something?"

"No, I'm afraid they were murdered in their home."

"What? Jesus Christ." He dragged his hands over his face. "I can't believe it. So that's why you were asking me where I was last night? You can't have actually thought I had anything to do with her dying?"

"When was the last time you saw Tabitha?" Erica asked. "Or had any kind of contact with her?"

He thought for a moment. "It's been a while. We haven't really needed to talk. Hang on, let me check my phone." He pulled it out of his pocket and scrolled until he reached what he wanted, then he turned the phone around and showed it to Erica and Shawn. "Those are our last messages." He let out a shaky sigh. "Christ, that sounds so final. I can't believe it."

"Do you mind if I take a photograph of that?" Erica nodded at the screen.

"Sure. I haven't got anything to hide."

She took a picture of the messages, though they didn't contain anything that raised any red flags. It was just friendly checking in with each other, asking how the other person was, and mentioning catching up soon. She didn't get the impression they'd left each other on bad terms.

"Tabitha didn't mention that she was worried about anything, or that someone had threatened her or was following her?"

"Nope. Nothing like that."

"How did the relationship between the two of you end?" Shawn asked.

"Honestly, it just kind of fizzled out. We'd been together so long, we'd got into a bit of a rut. She was the one who ended things. I was upset at the time, but deep down I knew she was right. We outgrew each other. I can't believe she's dead."

"I'm sorry for your loss," Erica said.

"What about Duke?" Reggie asked suddenly, sitting up straighter.

"Duke? The dog?"

"Yeah, our dog. I mean, Tabitha's dog now. He would have been there when she was…killed. Is he all right?"

"Yes, the dog is fine," she reassured him.

"What's happened to him? Where is he?"

"He's been taken by a dog handler and is now in kennels."

"I'll take him. I can't have him back in a rescue. That's where we got him from in the first place. He'll think he's been abandoned again."

"The two of you shared the pet when you were together?" She already knew this from what Tabitha's father had told her, but she wanted to make sure the story was true. Someone had got into the home without the dog barking, and there had to be a reason for that.

"Yes, look." He took a photo out of his wallet of him with the dog. "I let Tabitha take him because he was always closest to her, but it still broke my fucking heart. I won't let him stay in kennels. It's not right. He can come live with me."

Relocating a pet wasn't at the top of Erica's priorities right now, but she wouldn't want a dog to suffer unnecessarily. She was also aware that the animal was part of the investigation.

"We'll see what we can do," Shawn said. "We will also need to confirm with both your girlfriend and the takeaway that your story matches up."

"Go talk to her," Reggie said. "It's not like she's run off her feet."

Shawn stood. "What's her name?"

"Mirren Knight."

He exchanged a nod with Erica and then left them to speak to the girlfriend.

Erica took out her notepad. "I'm going to need the name of the takeaway, too."

"Sure. It's the Oriental Express on Fore Street. They'll probably know me by name. We order from there often enough. It's good. I can recommend it."

"I'm not sure they'll deliver to my part of London, but thanks."

Shawn turned away from the girlfriend, so Erica got to her feet and handed Reggie a card. "If anything comes up that might help us, will you let me know?"

"Of course. I want you to catch whatever bastard did this as much as you do."

Together, Erica and Shawn left the pub.

"What do you think of him?" she asked Shawn.

"Honestly, he seemed like a normal bloke. He was shocked when we broke the news, and the girlfriend can verify his story that he wasn't anywhere near the Moots' home last night."

"Unless she's covering for him."

"Possibly, but what's his motive? He seems to have moved on. The messages he showed us were amicable enough. I'm not getting any sense of him still hanging on to an old relationship, harbouring any grudges. Unless he's an excellent actor."

Erica agreed. "He seemed very open with the information he gave us. Maybe a bit too open? He's also the girlfriend's boss, and older than her by at least a decade. That could be enough sway to convince her to lie for him?"

"You're right. Plus, even if they went to bed when he said, he would have had time to sneak out, kill Tabitha and Jordon, and still get back home before his girlfriend woke up."

Erica considered this. "Let's see if we can get a location for his phone last night, too, make sure it matches his story, and send a couple of uniformed officers to his address to ask some neighbours in case he was spotted coming or going? I don't believe he's our guy, but it wouldn't be the first time I've been blindsided."

Chapter Eight

They walked back to the car.

It was getting late, and Erica really wanted to call it a night. Poppy was over at Natasha's place, and they would have already eaten dinner. She didn't like when she barely got home early enough to put Poppy to bed, but it couldn't be helped with big cases like this.

Her mobile rang, and she answered it. "DI Swift."

"Hi, it's DS Neale from the South Yorkshire Police. Sorry to call so late."

Erica stopped beside the car. "No problem."

"I've been speaking with Jordon Moots' family and friends today. I understand you're the SIO on the case?"

"Yes, that's right. How were Jordon's parents?"

"Devastated. Heartbroken. They couldn't think of any reason why someone might want to kill their son."

"So he didn't have any problems they were aware of? No issues with drugs or booze, or gambling?"

"No, nothing like that."

"When did they last see him?" she asked.

"They came down to visit a couple of months ago."

"It's been that long since they last saw each other?"

"Yeah, well, you know what they say about a daughter being for life, but a son only being a son until he gets a wife."

"That's sad," she said.

She bet they wished they'd all made more of an effort to see each other now. Maybe it was just natural for a son to distance himself from his parents—same as how male animals would in the wild. She didn't have a son. She didn't even have a brother, so she had no experience of it herself. Either way, she could almost guarantee the poor parents would beat themselves up about not making the most of the time they had left.

"Yes, it is. We're still tracking down some of his old school friends, trying to find out if they were in touch with Jordon recently, and if he may have said or done something that might indicate who is responsible."

"Okay. Stay in touch."

"Will do, Detective."

She ended the call and filled Shawn in on what had been said.

He shook his head. "No help there then?"

"No. Seems like these two were the perfect couple. No reason for anyone to want them dead."

Was there any possibility that Tabitha and Jordon had been picked out at random? That maybe a stranger saw them on the street and decided to target them? It was a possibility, but each time she considered this, she was brought back around to the violence of the attack. The hatred within it.

Though it was a completely different case, it reminded her of one she'd attended as a sergeant many years ago where a woman who'd suffered years of abuse at the hands of her husband had finally snapped one day. She'd been cooking dinner, and he'd tried to rape her up against the kitchen work surface, and she'd managed to get her hands on the knife she'd been using to chop up vegetables. During her interview, she said she'd blacked out, that she hadn't been aware of what she'd been doing, only that she'd wanted him to stop. She'd stabbed him twenty-seven times, and when the attending officers showed up on scene and said she was going to be arrested, she told them that was good. That she'd be happier in prison than she'd ever been at home.

But this wasn't a case of an abused woman finally snapping.

Had someone *else* snapped, though?

The two sides of this case warred inside her. How could someone have snapped while also meticulously planning a murder?

Chapter Nine

The following morning, as Erica stood by the coffee machine, wondering if she could stomach another coffee, Jon Howard approached.

"Boss, I've been looking into past cases that are similar to the current one, and I think I found something."

"Go on," she encouraged.

"There was a case that's similar, but it happened eighteen years ago. Same situation, a couple murdered in their home, the woman raped and stabbed to death in her bed. The husband was found in the living room, except it wasn't a glass that was smashed around him, it was a bone-china teacup."

"Did they arrest anyone for it?"

"Sure did. The wife's ex-partner. There was semen found inside the woman that matched his. He's always claimed his innocence. Said the two of them were having an affair, and that's why the semen was found, but that he hadn't laid a finger on her in violence, ever. He couldn't prove his whereabouts at the time of the murders, and someone was able to place him outside of the house the same evening the couple were killed. He always pleaded that he'd gone to the house in the hope of convincing the wife to come out and talk to him, said she was thinking of cooling things off, and he didn't want that. It took the jury three weeks to come to a decision, but in the end they decided he was guilty. He got a full life sentence."

"But he still maintains his innocence?"

"To this day, as far as I can tell."

Erica let the news sink in. "Was there ever any doubt in the case?"

Jon nodded. "There was DNA found at the scene that was never matched to anyone's, and the defence argued that the DNA belonged to the real killer, but something like that could never have been proven."

"What's the name of the man who was convicted?"

"Robert Brooks. He's in Belmarsh Prison."

Erica took a sip of the terrible coffee. "Did he have any family?"

"A mother and two sisters who campaigned for his release for many years. They all swore there was no way he would have done something like that."

"What happened to them?"

"The mother died ten years ago. One sister moved to Australia. The other is still around, I believe."

"Maybe we should talk to her, if we can. See what she thought of the whole thing."

"Good idea. I've sent you the case file so you can go over the crime scene photos. They're uncannily familiar."

"Thanks, Jon."

Erica carried her coffee back to her desk and opened up the old case file.

Could the cases be connected, or was she about to be led on a wild goose chase? She didn't like to believe in coincidences, but, looking at the old crime scene photos, she had to admit they were similar. What was going on with the smashed crockery and glassware? Had something been thrown during the attack? Why was it surrounding the men in both cases?

The profiles of the victims were also similar. Newly married, young, reasonably successful in their careers, so they could afford a nice home. She stared at the photos of the murdered couple and then brought them up to be side by side with Tabitha and Jordon Moots.

Even their appearances were similar.

But how could they have been murdered by the same person when the man convicted for the deaths of the couple eighteen years ago was still behind bars?

Unless this was a copycat killing. Or else Robert Brooks had never been the killer. If the killer was still out there, however, where had they been for the past eighteen years? There hadn't been any more murders, until now. Was the reason simply because the killer, Robert Brooks, had been behind bars all this time, or was it something darker?

There was one part of the case that hadn't fully added up; not even a single speck of blood had been found on Robert Brooks' body, hair, or clothes. Whoever had killed the couple must have been covered in blood. Looking at the crime scene images, it would have been everywhere. Of course, the prosecution argued that Brooks had simply done an excellent job of cleaning himself up. That he'd worn some kind of protective clothing, which he'd then burned or disposed of another way that had never been discovered. Trying to prove a defence case on something that wasn't present rather than something that was, was never going to be easy.

Would whoever had been responsible for the recent killings also have been covered in blood, or had they also used some protective clothing? It was hard to imagine someone walking through London, covered in blood, without someone noticing and, even if they hadn't called it in, would have taken a photograph or video and most likely posted it to social media. News of the horrific double murder had been all over the television and online, and she was sure if someone had seen something, they would have come forward by now.

She called a morning briefing to get everyone up to speed on developments. Unfortunately, other than the old case, there hadn't been much progress. No one seemed to have seen anything, and nothing had been caught on any local CCTV cameras either.

Hannah was compiling the couple's last movements from their phone and bank records, and Jon also had an appointment with Tabitha's boss that morning, to see if they could get a name of anyone who might be a suspect. They were also looking into the location of Reggie's phone to make sure his story was true.

Erica hoped to hear from either the pathologist or from forensics at some point today as well. She could do with a solid lead on this.

Before she let them get on with their actions, she went over the old case that Jon had found.

"Robert Brooks is currently spending a life-term sentence in Belmarsh Prison for the double murder, but I don't think we can ignore the similarities. I don't know what it means just yet, but we definitely need to compare all the DNA collected from the Moots' scene with samples taken from the older crime scene, see if anything matches up."

Shawn studied her from his seat. "You really think they might be connected?"

"Who knows," she said, "but we never ignore a lead."

Chapter Ten

Sadie didn't normally sleep with men on the first day of meeting them, but there was something different about Grant. They'd had an instant connection. He hadn't wanted to leave, and she hadn't wanted him to go either.

She still didn't have a front door key, but at least she had a spare key to her car so she could pick it up from where she'd abandoned it in the car park yesterday.

Plus, she still needed to get to her car.

"Mind if you give me a lift back into work?" she asked him. "Sorry if I'm putting you out...again."

"You're not putting me out, Sadie. If it means I get to spend more time with you, I'm happy."

They had to leave via the back door, and Sadie made sure she locked it behind her.

They reached Grant's car, and he pulled her in for a kiss like he couldn't keep his hands off her—his hands around her waist, his lips on hers. She felt like a teenager again. The neighbours were probably all curtain twitching, shaking their heads and rolling their eyes at the very public display of affection. She'd have probably done the same herself yesterday morning, but everything had changed now.

He brushed her hair away from her temple. "You're special, Sadie. You know that, right? From the first moment I saw you, I knew you were going to be someone important in my life."

"You can't have known that." She laughed.

"Well, I did. It was like being hit by lightning. I knew I'd never be the same again."

How was it possible that he'd come into her life less than twenty-four hours ago?

He drove them back to the car park where they'd met. She was relieved she had a yearly permit, or she'd be returning to find an expensive ticket or even her car towed.

"Aren't your colleagues going to notice you're still wearing the same shirt and suit?" she joked.

"Yep. Everyone in the office is going to want to know what I was doing last night."

"Maybe you should say that you got locked out of your flat."

"Yeah?" He kissed her again. "Or maybe I'll just tell them I got incredibly lucky."

She playfully thumped his shoulder. "You didn't strike me as a man who likes to kiss and tell."

"Sadie, baby, I want to tell the whole fucking world about you."

She even liked how he called her baby. Even Monty had liked him, choosing to sit on his lap, and purring, which Monty never did. Normally, if she had people around, Monty stayed as far away as possible.

"We really do have to go. I'm going to be late."

He checked his watch. "Shit, me, too. You've got my number, though. Call or text me. Whenever you want."

They forced themselves to part.

Was this really happening to her? She couldn't help but wonder if she was imagining things. If maybe this wasn't real, and he was just saying what she wanted to hear. That was possible, wasn't it? But the way he looked at her, the connection they had, she didn't think she was imagining any of that.

She spent the day at work on a high, practically floating down the corridors and smiling to herself at her desk. Even her colleagues commented on her good mood.

"Either you won the lottery or you met a man," one of the other solicitors, Nicola, commented.

"Maybe I did both?" she replied, feeling smug. "I had a knight in shining armour rescue me yesterday."

"Lucky you."

Her phone buzzed, and she checked the screen. It was a message from Grant, telling her how much he missed her already and how he couldn't believe she'd come into his life. She found herself grinning.

"Is that him?" Nicola asked.

"Yes, it is. He says he's missing me."

Her eyebrows lifted. "After one day? Doesn't that seem a bit...intense?"

"Honestly, the whole thing has been intense. I almost can't believe it's happening."

Nicola's lips thinned. "Just be careful."

"In what way? It's not as though he's asking me for money or anything."

"Not yet, he isn't."

"He has money. I don't need to worry about that."

Nicola exhaled through her nose. "You know nothing about this man."

"Not yet, I don't. But isn't that what this part is supposed to be about? The 'getting to know each other' part."

"Have you stalked him on social media yet? Made sure he is who he says he is?"

"No, of course not. I haven't even thought about it."

"Well, you should. Search up his name and where he lives. You might find a profile with photos of his wife and kids."

Sadie rolled her eyes. "Don't be so suspicious. Not everyone is like that. If he had a wife and kids, I highly doubt he'd have got away with spending all night with me. I didn't see him sneak off to make any weird phone calls or anything like that."

"I'm just saying to be cautious."

Sadie didn't like this conversation. She understood her coworker's concerns, but why couldn't it just be that something good was happening to her? Not everything in life needed to be bad. There were a lot of scammers around these days, but this was a whole different situation. She hadn't met him online. He wasn't some faceless username on the internet.

Sometimes love at first sight did happen.

"I'm seeing him again after work. I promise I'll get some more details from him then."

"Good. 'Cause if you're not going to internet stalk him, then I will."

Was she even a little bit curious? Maybe, but there was also a part of her that didn't want to know.

She wanted to stay cocooned in this bubble of happiness.

Sadie suddenly realised she couldn't social media stalk him even if she wanted to. How would she search him up?

She didn't even know his last name.

"What are you two gossiping about?" her boss, Tony, interrupted them. "I hope it's got to do with work."

Tony was in his early fifties and was an attractive bloke for his age, with salt-and-pepper hair. He sported a well-fitted suit designed around a body that was keeping middle-aged spread at bay with a few weekly gym sessions.

He'd once got drunk at an office party and cornered her while she was coming out of the toilets. He'd drunkenly confessed to her how he admired her and thought about her all the time. She'd managed to duck away from him and kept her distance the rest of the night. The next day he hadn't mentioned it, so she hadn't said anything either. She didn't know if he simply didn't remember or if they both preferred to act as though nothing had ever happened.

"Sadie's met a new man," Nicola piped up.

Sadie widened her eyes at her, trying to indicate her annoyance at Nicola throwing her under the bus. It really wasn't anyone else's business, and especially not her boss's. She already felt like they had a slightly awkward relationship. She always felt like she was going to say the wrong thing or that he was judging her badly for something. She wasn't sure how much of it was her own self-consciousness and chronic imposter syndrome, but even so, she definitely didn't want her personal life discussed with him.

He folded his arms across his chest, tightening the light-grey material of his suit jacket around his biceps, and angled his head to one side. "Is that so? I hope he's worth your time, Sadie."

"So do I. It's early days yet."

"*Very* early days," Nicola added.

Sadie thought that if Nicola tried to tell him that she'd slept with him the first day she'd met him, she might just take a swing for her colleague. Luckily, Nicola kept her mouth shut.

"Well, don't let it disturb your work," he said, jerking his chin at their desks. "You know how busy we are."

It was a clear comment to stop chinwagging and get back to the grind.

Sadie was relieved to be extradited from the conversation anyway and was happy to swing back around in her chair to face her desk again. She struggled to turn her thoughts back to work, however, her head buzzing with the events of the past twenty-four hours.

She felt stupid for not having put a spare front door key somewhere, or giving one to someone she trusted. Someone she trusted? She guessed that was part of the problem. She didn't really have anyone she trusted enough to give a front door key to. Problem was now that if the set of keys didn't show up, she was going to need to get a whole new lock put in. All she currently had was a back door key to let herself in and out of the flat. It was fine for the minute, but it wouldn't do long term.

She didn't like the thought that her other set of keys were still lost. Someone might have picked them up. She'd keep an eye out on the local Facebook groups, see if anyone had posted about finding them. Maybe she'd even do a post herself and see if she could locate them.

They had to be somewhere.

Chapter Eleven

Erica and Shawn stood outside the gates of Belmarsh Prison. This wasn't the first time she'd visited someone here, and she was sure it wouldn't be the last. She remembered when she'd come here several years ago to question the young man who'd murdered her husband, as well as harming numerous other people.

A chill ran over her skin. It was strange how something could simultaneously feel like yesterday and also feel like a lifetime ago. She'd grown and changed so much since then. Now Poppy was a preteen, and Erica was in a new relationship. She hoped her husband would be looking down on her and approved of what she'd done with her life.

They both showed their ID to the prison officer in the entrance booth, and they went through the routine of pat-downs and had a sniffer-dog brought up to them. Then they were buzzed in, and a second officer came to meet them.

"We're here to speak to Robert Brooks," she told him.

"Yeah, I've been sent down to take you through."

"What's he like?" she asked.

"Decent kind of bloke," the officer replied, surprising her. "Quiet. Introverted. Keeps himself to himself, most of the time. Not had any problems with him."

"He's convicted of brutally murdering two people."

"I know that." He seemed to shrug it off.

Erica and Shawn exchanged a glance. Erica guessed that when you were around murderers and rapists all day, every day, you got immune to it. The prison officers stopped seeing the inmates as the crimes they'd been committed for and saw them as people.

It was different as a police officer. She was what came before the conviction. Their job was to find these people and do what was needed to ensure they ended up behind bars and couldn't hurt anyone again. Once that was done, she did her best to put that criminal out of her mind because there was always a new one to have to deal with. A new criminal. A new crime. She'd already handed the old one over to the prison service.

They were led through the prison, to one of the rooms where prisoners were allowed to speak in private with their solicitors. They'd already booked the appointment, so the prison officers had known they were coming and had prepared both the room and the prisoner ready for their arrival.

The prison had such a distinctive smell—boiled cabbage mixed with teenage boys' changing rooms. Once more, she was taken back to when she'd come here to visit her husband's killer. It was like stepping back in time, and a part of her brain tried to convince her that on the other side of that door, Nicholas Bailey would be sitting, waiting for her.

Nicholas Bailey was dead. That wasn't going to happen.

Shawn pinched his lips together and frowned at her. "You okay? You've gone pale."

She blew out a breath. "Yeah, just my mind playing tricks on me."

"I can go in alone," he offered. "You don't need to be here. It's probably beneath your pay grade anyway."

"No, it's fine. I'm fine. I like to look into their eyes. See if they're telling the truth for myself."

"I get it. But speak up if you change your mind."

"I will," she promised.

Robert Brooks was sitting on the other side of the table. He was in his fifties now, but his slender arms knotted and wiry with muscle indicated that he spent time in the gym. His hair was greying and thinning at the crown. His blue eyes appeared sharp behind his black-framed glasses.

His hands were cuffed, and the cuffs attached to a metal hoop in the middle of the table. Was Robert Brooks still a violent man? Erica couldn't imagine he was going anywhere. They'd been buzzed through numerous locked gates on the way here. No one was getting away.

"Mr Brooks," Erica said, taking a seat opposite. "I'm DI Swift, and this is my colleague, DS Turner. Thank you for taking the time to speak to us."

"It's not like I don't have plenty of it to spare," he said.

It was hard to believe this man was responsible for the brutal murder of two innocent people. She had seen those old crime scene photos, and they'd been shocking. Both victims had been stabbed multiple times. Whoever had killed them had been in a frenzy, yanking the blade from the bodies and plunging it in again, over and over.

Shawn sat, too. "Do you know why we're here, Mr Brooks?"

"Not the details, no. I was only told you wanted to speak to me in connection with the murder of my ex and her husband."

"That's correct," Erica said.

He linked his fingers on the table and looked between Erica and Shawn. "I'm afraid I'm going to disappoint you, Detectives."

Erica arched her eyebrows. "Oh, in what way?"

"I can't give you any more information on the two murders than you'll be able to read in the case files. Whatever little details you're hoping I'll corroborate I won't be able to do because I wasn't there."

"You're sticking by your story that you're innocent?" she asked.

"It's not a story. I *am* innocent. I never would have hurt her. Never. I loved her."

It was hard to picture this mild-mannered man slaughtering those people. But the killings had happened years ago, and he'd been a young man then. He'd most likely been a different man then, too. Spending a lifetime behind bars changed a person.

Erica folded her hands on the table between them. "What are you saying? That whoever killed her might still be out there?"

"And has done it again?" He must have noted her expression, a muscle at the corner of his mouth twitching. "Don't be surprised, Detective. We still get to watch the news in here. You must have realised I'd have noticed the similarities between the two cases."

"We're keeping our minds open," Erica said. "It's early days in the investigation."

"But that's why you're here," he pressed. "You understand that if the same person killed that couple yesterday as killed Beatrice and Jack Gabriel eighteen years ago, then it couldn't have been me."

"It's possible this is a copycat murder," Shawn said.

Robert pressed his lips together and glanced down. "I see. That would be convenient. It would mean your lot didn't get it wrong when they arrested and charged me."

"You were convicted," Erica reminded him. "That was down to a judge and a jury."

"Maybe so, but I didn't do it. The person who did is still out there. Perhaps, even after all this time, they decided they wanted to do it again."

"Was there anyone you thought was guilty at the time? Anyone you believed the police should point the finger at?"

He shook his head. "I wish I had a name for you, but I don't."

"How do you do it?" Shawn asked. "Let's assume what you're saying is true, and you are locked up for life when you're an innocent man, how do you stop yourself going crazy?"

He closed his eyes briefly, as though centring himself, before opening them again. "I'm not angry anymore. I was, for a very long time. I was fucking furious. I thought the rage might drive me insane, and I think a part of me wanted to go insane because then I wouldn't understand what was happening to me anymore. I was grieving for Beatrice as well; I wanted to kill whoever it was who raped and murdered her. I can't even tell you what it feels like to be so utterly fucking helpless."

"How did you get over it?"

"I found God." He smiled almost sheepishly. "I know it's a cliché, but it is what it is. I gave myself over to Him, trusted that He had some purpose for me I didn't yet understand. It helped with the anger. I stopped trying to find someone to blame and fighting to get my name cleared. There wasn't any point—it was never going to happen. The years went by, and I grew older and calmer, and I saw all these young men come into the prison, filled with that same kind of rage I had, and I decided it was my job to work with them." He gave a gruff laugh. "I'm not going to say I helped all of them. The vast majority told me to fuck off, but I helped some, and that was enough."

Erica wasn't sure what to think. Robert certainly came across as a genuine person, but plenty of people in prison were excellent liars.

They thanked Robert for his time and left the prison.

"Well, that was a waste of time," Erica said. "He didn't give us anything to go on."

Shawn exhaled a huff of air. "What's he got to gain from continuing to express his innocence?"

"Early release?"

"He doesn't seem like he's after an early release, and considering the amount of time he's spent inside, nothing could really be thought of as early at this point."

Erica considered his point. "Maybe he's delusional. He's spent so many years trying to convince everyone of his innocence that now he believes it himself. He was convicted for a reason. He had motive and was placed at the scene, and there was his DNA on her body. Yes, he might have had reasons for those things, but the reason could have just as easily been that it was because he raped and murdered her."

"But what if he is actually innocent? Can you imagine spending a whole lifetime in prison for a murder you didn't commit?"

She gave a grim smile. "I don't think I'd be quite so calm."

"It's taken him approaching twenty years to get to that place."

They fell into a comfortable silence, both contemplating the life of Robert Brooks.

"If we are looking at a copycat killer," Shawn said, "why copy a case that took place eighteen years ago?"

Erica twisted her lips. "I have no idea."

The ring of her phone drew her attention. The pathologist's name, Lucy Kim, appeared on the screen.

Erica glanced over at Shawn.

"I guess they're ready for us down at the morgue."

Chapter Twelve

The lock clicked in Liam's bedroom door.

He sat up straight, his ears straining.

"Dad?"

No response came to his call, and Liam listened hard for the sound of the front door shutting behind him.

Was his father going out? It was happening more and more recently—his dad going out and leaving him locked in the house alone.

Liam worried about what would happen if there was a fire and he was the only one here. He had no access to a phone or the internet, unless he had his father's supervision. His dad let him go online—encouraged it even—but only to look at the sites his father wanted him to read.

It didn't matter that he didn't have access to a phone, though he'd have felt better in case of an emergency. It wasn't as though he had any friends to call anyway. He'd been homeschooled ever since he'd been old enough to read. The idea of being in a normal school, surrounded by other people, terrified him. Even if he went to an all-boys' school, there would be women there, too, in the form of teachers.

Dad had warned him his whole life about women. About how evil and cruel and vile they were. They did terrible, disgusting things. They would want to do terrible, disgusting things to him.

Liam remembered the conversation he'd had with his father.

He'd grabbed Liam's chin, squeezing painfully between his thumb and forefinger. "We're at war, boy," he'd said. "Do you understand that? War. And do you know what war is? It's violent, and bloody, and forces you to do things that make you question your morals. But we're not the bad men in this. We're the ones who are ridding the world of its evil."

"I understand," Liam had replied.

"I know you feel isolated here, maybe sometimes even alone, but we're not alone. You've seen the message boards and the sites. We're rising up. We're changing things. Can't you see how important that is? How it needs to be the reason we live and breathe?" His father had shaken his head. "You know, I envy you sometimes. I've kept you so sheltered here in this house. Maybe too much. I've only done it because I love you. I've wanted to protect you from them, and I've tried, I really have."

"I know, Dad."

He'd released Liam's chin and ruffled his hair instead. "It makes me proud that you understand."

Liam wanted to make his dad proud. It was what he wanted most in the world. If his father told him he should be frightened of these people, then he would be. His dad was big and strong, and Liam felt like nothing should ever scare him. In fact, he hadn't seen any evidence of him being frightened. If anything, it was the people he came across who were frightened of him, but then Liam guessed that was what his dad wanted.

Even so, Liam had had questions. "Didn't you have a mum? What was she like? Was she bad, too?"

"You don't want to know what kind of person my mother was," his father had replied. "She was sick in the head, Liam.

Rotten right through. You know when you see a piece of fruit that is perfect on the outside, but then you take a bite, and the inside is brown and rotten, that's what she was like."

"What about your father—my grandfather? Didn't he understand what she was?"

"No. Her beauty blinded him to it, just like all these women think they can get away with. Why do you think they paint their faces? It's a mask meant to trick us. Even the ugly ones think they can get away with it. They're laughing at us, Liam. They even post videos on social media boasting about how easy it is to turn themselves from disgusting creatures into evil seductresses. It sickens me. They force men to fall in love with them and then they bleed them for everything they have. Fucking vampires, Liam, that's what they are. Excuse my language. It's better that you grow up understanding who they are and what needs to happen than finding out for yourself. If you let one get their claws into you, they'll destroy you."

"So you hurt them instead?"

"It's the only way. One day, you'll understand that I have no choice in what I do. I can't just sit back and let them get away with what they're doing to us."

Liam had frowned with confusion. "It's not only the women you're eradicating, though. It's the men, too."

"Some men aren't the same as us," his dad had said.

"I don't understand. Aren't they being tricked by the women in the same way?"

"No, because they look down on us, too. Just because they got fortunate when it came to genetics, they think they're somehow above the rest of us. We need to prove that we're not the weaker part of society. If it means these men are taken down at the same time, then so be it."

Liam hadn't pushed his father any further, just in case his dad suddenly decided that Liam was one of those men, too.

Sometimes, the conversations left him feeling kind of icky and squeamish inside, but he tried not to pay any notice to that. He was happy just to have Dad's attention. He didn't get any other interaction.

All he had was his books, ones his father chose for him. Even they were filled with stories about how awful women could be.

He didn't remember his mother. When he'd been younger, and realised he had one out there somewhere, he'd made the mistake of asking his father who she was. That had resulted in him being locked in his room with nothing to eat for three days. Before he'd been locked in, his father had told him exactly what he thought of the woman who'd birthed him. She was a whore, he'd said. A money-grabbing slut. She'd spread her legs, thinking it would tie him to her, but once she'd got pregnant, everything had changed.

He said if the baby had been a girl, he'd have drowned it in the bath.

Liam was glad he hadn't been born a girl.

Liam was used to entertaining himself. He'd been doing it for years now. He told himself he didn't need anyone else's company—no one but his dad anyway. He prided himself on his vivid imagination, how he could spend hours lying on his bed on his back, picturing himself in the places he read about in his books. Sometimes, his dad let him watch the television in the living room with him in the evenings. Those were the best times. His dad would even bring him home a treat, like popcorn or chocolate, or the super-sour gummy sweets Liam loved.

While they were watching TV, his dad talked to him about all the terrible things that had happened in the world and the people who were at fault. It made Liam feel special, that his dad would confide in him about the things that bothered him, and Liam always agreed with everything he said.

Now he just had to wait for his dad to come back and tell him what they needed to do next.

His dad always had the answers to everything.

Chapter Thirteen

The morgue wasn't one of Erica's favourite places. She couldn't understand how someone would want to spend all day, every day here. Today the smell of the place seemed even worse than usual. It didn't normally bother her, but she found herself happy to pull on the protective gear, including a mask to cover her mouth and nose.

"And how have you been?" Lucy Kim, the pathologist, asked her.

Lucy's latest hairstyle was shaved on one side, a purple streak down her jaw-length black hair on the other. "That daughter of yours must be almost grown by now."

Erica laughed. "Not quite, though she acts like a teenager half the time. I'm not sure how I'm going to cope with her when she actually is one. She's going to give me a few more grey hairs, I'm sure."

"Pssh, you don't have any grey hairs, and I'm sure she'll be fine. She's got you as a mum, hasn't she? What better role model could she have?"

Erica found her cheeks warming at the compliment. "Thanks, I hope you're right."

"She's right," Shawn assured her.

Erica flapped her hand in front of her face. "Now the two of you are embarrassing me. Don't we have some dead bodies to look at?"

Even observing the dead would be more comfortable than receiving praise on her parenting skills. Her mothering skills were something she'd always questioned herself about. Always torn between being a good mum to Poppy while also being a good detective. If she hadn't had the amount of support from her sister over the years, she knew she'd never have been able to raise a child while having such a demanding job.

Two of the metal examination tables were occupied, sheets covering the bodies.

"You're still enjoying spending your days with dead bodies, then, Lucy?" Erica said.

"They make better company than the living. They're excellent listeners and don't give me an argument about too much."

"About too much? That makes it sound like they give you an argument every now and then?"

"They do," Lucy agreed. "When they won't give up their secrets. When I know there's more going on with their death than their remains are telling me, that's when we fall out."

Erica laughed. "I know that feeling. How about my two victims? They holding anything back from you?"

"Other than telling me exactly who killed them? I don't think so. You saw the state of the bodies? While I never like to assume anything, it seems fairly clear to me what the cause of death was."

"Multiple stab wounds?" Erica suggested.

"Exactly. Let's take a closer look at the female victim."

Lucy pulled the sheet back, revealing Tabitha Moots' body.

"As you already know," Lucy said, "I saw these bodies in situ and took multiple samples from their skin before the bodies were moved. The number of injuries and the amount of blood certainly made my job that much harder."

"They were extremely violent attacks," Erica agreed.

"I never make assumptions about how a person died, however. While it's clear these victims have been stabbed multiple times, there's also the possibility they were dead before they were stabbed, and the knife wounds are someone's way of covering up what really happened. I did see the crime scene and noted the blood spatter patterns, so I'd say that isn't the case here. I've run tox screens on both of them. There was a small volume of alcohol in both their systems, but that was all. No signs that they'd been drugged."

It bothered Erica that this person or persons was able to stab both Tabitha and Jordon to death without anyone hearing anything. Why hadn't they screamed for help? Unless there were two perpetrators, had one of the victims just stayed put while their spouse was being stabbed? Why would they have done that, and not run and tried to escape, or attacked the killer and tried to stop them?

"Already having their identity is helpful," Lucy carried on. "We know she's a thirty-one-year-old Caucasian female, fifty-four kilos and a hundred and sixty-two centimetres in height. I was able to use her medical history to dig deeper into her background. No known pregnancies. No ongoing medical issues that we're aware of. She was a healthy young woman. I took DNA samples, blood samples, and her prints. We always want to have them on file for comparison."

"Sure," Erica said.

"I started my examination by taking scans of the body, looking for broken bones or anything that was out of the ordinary—such as recent operations. Then I checked the surface of the skin for fluids, bruising, scars, or abrasions. As well as the stab wounds, she has injuries consistent with being raped."

"Was the sexual assault pre or postmortem?" Shawn asked.

"He raped her while she was still alive. Did he also rape her afterwards? That's impossible to say. She was found facedown on the bed. The spatter pattern on the mattress, floor, and walls suggest she was alive when the stabbing started. From the postmortem lividity, the way the blood has pooled in the lower parts of the body, I'd say she wasn't moved. She was killed where she was found."

"Poor woman," Erica muttered.

Lucy continued, "In total, I counted twenty-six stab wounds for the female victim. I've documented each one of them. They range from deep penetrating stabs to more superficial gashes, perhaps where she was struggling and the knife didn't quite meet its mark."

Erica looked up at her. "Any idea what kind of blade was used?"

"From the shape of the stab wounds, I'd say the blade was un-serrated. Obviously, the size of a wound doesn't directly relate to the length of the blade. I can only tell you the depth of the deepest wound. The width is also only an estimate, since skin stretches when it is cut and contracts again once the blade is removed."

"I understand," Erica said.

Lucy produced a diagram of the torso. Figures in small, neat handwriting had been attached to marks drawn on the figure. It was clear each mark and the number related to a knife wound on the female victim and the size and depth of it.

"The six deepest puncture marks to the epigastric area and the hypogastric area are most likely the wounds that killed her." Lucy indicated to a mark on the body. "Do you see the shape of the wound—how the wound has one sharp end and one flat end? That's because it's from a one-sided blade. There is also bruising around the wound which tells me it was a knife that had a hilt."

"We're still searching for the knife," Shawn said. "We didn't locate it in the home, which means the killer took it with him. Whether he disposed of it along the way or still has it as some kind of memento, unfortunately, we'd don't yet know. The location of the home is near the canal, so the killer could have tossed it. It's helpful to know exactly what we need to be watching out for."

"From the direction of the blade wounds," Lucy said, "I'd say the attacker was leaning over the top of her, bringing the blade down in a stabbing motion. The person holding the knife was most likely right-handed."

"That doesn't help us narrow it down much," Shawn said.

Lucy glanced up at him. "I believe he carried on stabbing her long after she'd died."

Erica nodded slowly, considering this. "When I saw the crime scene, the first thing I thought was that there was a lot of anger involved in the killing. It was a passionate crime."

Lucy raised her eyebrows. "You think the couple were known to their killer?"

"That's what my gut is telling me, but who knows. We're keeping all possibilities open right now. Did she fight back at all? Is there any chance we'll get the killer's DNA from under her nails?"

"There was no obvious sign of skin or blood, but I've taken samples, so we might get something."

"What about traces of semen?"

"No, but I found spermicide in the vaginal walls."

"You think he used a condom?" Shawn asked.

"I believe so, yes."

"What did he do with the used condom once he was done?" Erica was thinking out loud.

"Maybe he took that with him, too?" Shawn suggested. "Could be in the same place as the knife?"

Lucy grimaced. "From what I can tell, he's done a good clean-up job. Or at least done what he needed to keep his own DNA from being left behind."

Erica adjusted her gloves. "It's early days yet. He'll have missed something. They always do."

Erica walked over to where Jordon Moots lay in the exact same pose as his wife. How tragic that this young couple, who, it seemed, had everything going for them, came to such a violent end. Why would someone want them dead, and so viciously, too?

Lucy Kim joined Erica.

"There are far fewer stab wounds on the male victim. Eight in total, with only three causing penetrating abdominal trauma. The cause of death is haemorrhagic shock from the incisions to his small bowel, liver, and intra-abdominal vasculature."

"Any sign of ligature marks or fibres around his wrists or ankles?" Erica asked.

Lucy shook her head. "No. Why do you ask?"

"I just find it strange that neither of them tried to run or even call out for help. There's a possibility there were two perpetrators, one keeping the other victim still and silent while the killer did what he wanted."

Chapter Fourteen

Erica came away from the postmortem feeling as though other than the approximate size and shape of the knife used to murder the couple, she hadn't really learned anything she hadn't already known.

"You're quiet," Shawn said.

"Sorry, just thinking. We could do with a solid lead on this one."

"We still might get a hit on the DNA samples taken."

"Hopefully."

For some reason she didn't think that was going to happen. Had the killer worn some kind of protective gear similar to what they wore going into a crime scene? The killer had gained entry to the flat knowing exactly what he was going to do. He had taken the time to cover his hair and had most likely worn gloves. He'd even taken some condoms with him. How had he got into the flat, and why hadn't the dog barked?

Each time she asked herself these questions, she came back to the same thing. The killer was known to the couple. That was the reason the dog hadn't barked—the dog was already friendly with the killer.

Back at the office, a man was waiting for Erica.

"I'm one of Jordon's friends—" He caught himself. "I mean, I *was* one of Jordon's friends."

"Come through," she invited him. "Let's find somewhere private where we can talk."

She checked the interview rooms and found one empty. She keyed in the code, and it beeped open, and she led him through and gestured for him to sit.

"I'm sorry, but I didn't catch your name."

"Ty Grogan," he said.

"How long have you known Jordon?"

"A couple of years. We met at the gym and got talking, and then discovered we both liked footie, so we watched a game and grabbed a pint together. That was pretty much the basis of our friendship, but we were good mates, you know." He pinched his lips together, his eyes growing glassy.

"Can you think of anyone who might have wanted to harm Jordon?"

Ty seemed troubled. "I didn't know if I should even say something. It was a while ago, and it probably has nothing to do with the murders."

Erica linked her fingers on the table. "How about you tell me what it is and let us be the judge of that."

"Jordon had a stalker ex-girlfriend when him and Tabitha first got together."

"What do you mean by stalker? That sounds serious."

"Maybe I used the word wrongly," he said and then he hesitated. "Actually, no, I didn't. He finished with her and then started to go out with Tabitha only a couple of weeks after. This girl wasn't happy about it at all. She'd show up at his flat in the middle of the night, banging on his door and crying and screaming. She'd wait for him outside of his work and accost him then. She even went for Tabitha one time, calling her a whore and all sorts of horrible things. I remember Jordon thought Tabitha was going to break up with him about it, but she didn't. They were perfect for each other."

"What happened to the ex?" Erica asked.

"Eventually, she got the idea and stopped hassling them."

"Do you know her name?"

"It was Anna, or might have been Emma. Something like that."

Erica chewed on her lower lip. "Any surname?"

He pulled a face. "No, sorry."

They weren't going to get very far on only a couple of first names that might not even be correct. She made a mental note to contact the detective in Sheffield to find out if the parents knew of a previous girlfriend.

"Did Jordon ever call the police?" she asked.

"No. Jordon was a decent bloke. I think he felt sorry for her. He knew he'd broken her heart, and he still cared about her, even if he didn't want to be with her anymore. He didn't want to get her in trouble."

"Do you know if they'd been in touch recently? Reconnected at all?"

"Not that I'm aware of. Jordon wouldn't go behind Tabitha's back to hook up with an ex, if that's what you're thinking. He was a really decent guy, and he loved Tabitha. He wouldn't have gone back to his ex-girlfriend."

"Was she ever violent towards him or Tabitha?"

"Yeah, a couple of times, but not in a 'stabbing them to death' kind of way. I think he had to restrain her when they broke up because she went for him, holding her arms away 'cause she was trying to slap and scratch him."

Erica thought for a moment. "Do you have any photographs of her?"

"No, but there might be some old ones on Jordon's social media. Unless he's deleted them, of course, which he might have done."

"Okay, thanks, Ty. Have you got a phone number, in case I need to speak to you again?"

He wrote it down for her, and she showed him back out of the station.

Erica took what she'd learned to Shawn.

"You don't think there's anything in it, do you?" Shawn asked. "We know a male was responsible for the murders. Tabitha was raped."

"Or are we making assumptions? Maybe it wasn't the murderer who raped her. Maybe someone else had raped her earlier in the day, and then a different person broke in and killed them both."

Shawn raised his eyebrows. "And that someone was a woman? A woman overcame two people and then stabbed them both to death?" His disbelief was evident.

"Don't get blindsided by making assumptions. We know Tabitha was stabbed eighteen times more than Jordon. To me that says whoever held the knife really hated Tabitha. This person knew the couple's dog, maybe even had their own key."

"And you think that person might have been his ex-girlfriend?"

"Maybe they had something going on behind Tabitha's back? Or maybe the ex-girlfriend had an accomplice? We simply don't know right now, which is why we need to talk to her."

Shawn steepled his fingers to his lips. "If Jordon was in contact with his ex, it'll show up on his phone records or via messages on his laptop or iPad."

"Good, because right now, we don't even know who she is."

Chapter Fifteen

As Sadie trotted down the steps from the office, a car horn tooted.

She glanced over to discover Grant waiting for her in his car. A smile broke across her face, and she lifted her hand in a wave.

He climbed out from behind the wheel and stood beside the driver's door.

She crossed the car park, clutching her handbag strap with her opposite hand so her arm created a barrier across her chest.

A wave of shyness and self-consciousness swept over her. Fear that she had imagined the intensity of the connection, or that it was all one-sided, filled her.

But Grant took her hand and kissed her. "I've been thinking about you all day."

She grinned with happiness. "I've been thinking about you, too."

"It felt like the longest working day of my life. I swear, I couldn't wait for it to be over so I could see you again."

She was conscious of people looking, of her work colleagues probably gossiping behind her back.

"Let's get out of here, shall we?" she said.

"Where do you want to go?"

She glanced down at her work outfit. "I'm not sure, but before I do anything, I need to get out of these clothes."

He smirked. "Sounds like a good plan to me."

She couldn't help laughing. "I do need to drive my car, though. Will you follow me home?"

"I'll follow you wherever you want me to."

"Thanks, Grant."

Already, she was starting to wonder what she would do without him. She shook the thought from her head. That was crazy talking. She barely knew the bloke, and she needed to slow down. She didn't want to prove Nicola right.

Then again, maybe they would both prove Nicola wrong. It happened, didn't it? People met and fell madly in love and went on to live long and happy lives together. It might not happen all the time, but she'd bet she could find some examples with just a quick internet search. It wasn't as though she'd had much luck in the past with relationships. Perhaps that was because Lady Luck had been saving it all up because meeting Grant had always been in Sadie's future.

She knew she was getting silly and fanciful, but she couldn't help herself.

It was lucky that she'd remembered to pick up the spare key that morning.

She got in, started the engine, and pulled out onto the road. She checked her rear-view mirror to make sure he was still following her. He was.

Driving in London traffic at this time of the day was hellish. It wasn't easy making sure he didn't lose her, though she assumed he'd be able to find his way, if she did. People drove aggressively, cutting in front of her or merging into a lane where there wasn't really any space. Somehow, he managed to stay on her tail, and less than thirty minutes later, she stopped outside her flat.

He found a place to park a little farther down the road.

"Made it," he said, breaking into a jog to reach her. He tugged her towards him and kissed her again.

"Let me go and get changed," she said, "and then we can do something. Do you want to grab dinner somewhere?"

"That means being out in public?"

She gave a small laugh. "You don't want to be out in public?"

"I don't want to share you with anyone else. How about we get a takeaway and eat it in bed?"

Sadie was mildly horrified at the thought. "I am not eating dinner in bed. How slovenly do you think I am?"

"I have no idea, but I can't wait to find out."

She realised he was wearing a different shirt. "Oh, you got changed?"

"Yeah, I slipped out during my lunch hour so I could get a clean set of clothes."

"You didn't plan on going home then?"

He winced. "Is that too presumptuous of me? I didn't mean to—"

She cut him off. "No, no, it's fine. I promise. I'm glad you're here. I didn't want you to go home either."

He held her gaze. "That's good then. I'm glad we're on the same page."

She jerked her head towards her flat. "Come on, let's go inside. We still have to use the back door, though. There's no sign of my keys. I might have to think about changing the lock."

Sadie still wanted to shower and change, even if they were planning on staying home. She felt stale from the day sat at her desk and wanted to freshen up. Before she did anything else, though, she wanted a cup of tea and decided it was only right for her to offer him one as well.

They went into the kitchen, and she reached for the kettle and paused, her hand midair.

The water in the kettle was almost half full. She never filled the kettle that high. Even when she had company, she only boiled the amount she needed. She'd bought a clear kettle that had cup markings on the side. She'd boiled it that morning, and made coffee, so there shouldn't even be any water in there, never mind it being almost half full.

Curious, she placed her palm to the side of the kettle. Could she feel some residual warmth? Or was she imagining things?

Her stomach flipped with unease.

She glanced over her shoulder at Grant. "You didn't come back here, did you?"

His brow tightened in a frown. "No, of course not. I've been at work all day and it's not like I have a key. Why do you ask?"

"The kettle," she said, feeling silly, "it has water in it."

"So?"

"I never fill it that much."

"Oh, I must have filled it this morning, before we left."

"Why would you do that?"

He shrugged. "I don't know. Save you a job when you got home and fancied a cuppa? It's not a big deal, is it?"

"No, it's just that I try not to waste either water or the energy it takes to boil the water if it's not going to be used. It's bad for the environment and it's a waste of money."

She was being a prude. She didn't want him to look at her any differently, and a tight-arse hippy wasn't the impression she wanted to make.

She shook her head and clicked the kettle on to boil, deliberately not emptying out the excess water so she didn't seem like a crazy person. "It doesn't matter." She wanted to change the subject, reflect it back onto him. "Where *do* you work anyway? You never told me."

"Yes, I did."

"No, you said *what* you did for work, but not where."

"Aah, right. Sorry. It's probably 'cause it's not that exciting. It's just an office block down in Holborn."

"What were you doing in the car park near my work yesterday? It's a bit out of your way, isn't it?"

He cocked his head. "What's with the twenty questions, Sadie?"

"Sorry. It's just my coworkers were worried about me, you know, hooking up with you when we'd only just met. I told them that we had a connection and they didn't have anything to worry about, but they seemed to think that kind of thing was exactly what a scammer would want a person to think."

"Do you really think I'm a scammer?"

Her cheeks flushed with heat, and she squirmed inside her skin. Saying it out loud made it sound ridiculous. This wasn't going well at all. Maybe yesterday really had been a one-off. "No, of course I don't."

He gestured towards her. "Because I could just as easily say the same about you."

This annoyed her. "Not really. You were the one who approached me, remember?"

"Are we having our first fight, Sadie?" He was teasing her now.

She preferred that to the idea of them actually having an argument. He could walk away from her, and that would be it. They'd be done. They had nothing connecting them. No past history or current ties. She didn't want to lose him.

She took his hand. "Ignore me. We're not fighting. It was just my stupid colleagues putting thoughts into my head."

"It's good they're watching out for you, but don't listen to them in future. I know this is fast, but it's also right. They can't know or understand how it is to fall for someone like you. You're so perfect, Sadie. I wish you could see yourself through my eyes."

She shook her head and glanced away. "Believe me, I'm far from perfect."

He caught her by the chin and stared into her eyes. "Well, you're perfect to me."

Should she tell him what had happened when she was twelve years old? How she'd been the one to find her sister hanging from the lampshade in their shared room? Should she tell him how she'd screamed and then thrown up, but how she hadn't done anything to help? Maybe her sister had still been alive at that point, and she could have stopped her from dying if she'd only grabbed her legs to relieve the pressure, or placed the toppled stool back under her feet. Should she tell him how her mother had screamed and rushed in to help, or how her father had yelled at the nine-nine-nine operator down the phone?

Instead of letting all that horror out of her mouth, she kept her lips clamped shut. No one needed to hear about all of that, especially not a man who was looking at her the way he was. He didn't need to know how she'd barely eaten for over a year after it had happened, how she'd dropped so much weight she'd appeared skeletal, and her hair had started to fall out. She'd missed a whole year of school—not that it had mattered much. She'd still gone on to get outstanding exam results. After everything that had happened, she'd felt she'd owed it to both her dead sister and her parents. If only her mother had lived long enough to see what she'd done with her life. Would she be proud? Would her sister?

She didn't want to think about all that right now. Even with it being so many years later, she still found her eyes prickling with tears at the memories. She didn't want Grant to ask her what was wrong, worried he'd think she was getting upset about the stupid kettle, and so busied herself with making the tea.

"Here," she said, handing his mug to him. "You okay if I leave you for a minute to go and jump in the shower?"

He put his cup down on the side. "Sure you don't want some company?" He wrapped his arms around her waist.

A smile touched the corners of her lips. "Actually, that sounds like a lot more fun than being alone."

Chapter Sixteen

Erica woke the following morning not feeling so great. She'd eaten that shop-bought sandwich the previous day and had thought it hadn't smelled great. She was normally careful about what she ate, aware she simply didn't have the time to get food poisoning, but her stomach definitely wasn't doing well this morning. She felt a little like she was travel sick, though she'd only managed to get from the bed to the bathroom so far.

Shawn was already downstairs. The cheerful sound of him preparing breakfast for Poppy and helping to get her ready for school drifted up the stairs.

She checked her phone to see if there had been any developments in the case overnight, but it seemed everything had been quiet. At least the killer hadn't struck again. She wasn't sure how she'd handle things if she had to go to a new crime scene this morning. She normally prided herself on her strong stomach but had the feeling things would be different today.

She went downstairs to join them in the kitchen.

"You okay?" Shawn asked her, frowning. He paused mid-action, his spoon lifted halfway between his bowl and his mouth.

"Yeah, just reminding myself that it's never a good idea to eat a tuna sandwich from a garage."

"Oh damn. You okay to work?"

"Yeah, I'll be fine. Just feeling a little delicate."

"Think you can manage some toast? It might help settle your stomach?"

"Thanks. I'll give it a go."

Poppy pulled a face at Erica. "Eww, did you throw up?"

"No, I didn't. I felt like it, though. Thanks for being so sympathetic."

"I hate it when people throw up. It makes me want to puke, too."

"Well, we can't have that, can we? Last thing I need is you vomiting all over the place."

Shawn put down his spoon. "You guys are really making me enjoy my breakfast."

Erica couldn't help laughing. "Sorry."

He got to his feet. "Sit down, and I'll make you that toast."

She turned to the subject of work while he fed a slice of white bread into the toaster. "I don't think there have been any developments on the case overnight. Have you heard anything different?"

He shook his head. "No, though I'm not sure if that's good or bad."

The trouble with living with someone you also worked with meant that it was hard keeping the boundaries of work life and home life separate.

Shawn hadn't officially moved in. He still had his own place, where he kept the majority of his belongings, but he spent most nights at her house. It was important they kept up appearances, and it wasn't as though Shawn could change his address to hers anytime soon. Doing so would certainly make people in the office ask questions.

She was conscious that she didn't want Poppy overhearing too much of what was being said, though Poppy was old enough to find out information for herself now. She'd be starting secondary school in only a matter of months, and Erica had finally relented on Poppy having her own phone, though Erica made sure she had the passwords to everything and checked the contents on a regular basis. As much as Erica didn't like it, phones and the internet were simply a part of life these days, and she'd rather Poppy learned how to use them responsibly and was overseen by parental guidance than Poppy hitting her teenage years and going crazy with it. Phones were also the way all the kids stayed in touch these days, and to not allow Poppy to be a part of it meant she'd be a social outcast with many of her friends at school. That didn't mean Erica was one hundred percent happy about it, however. In a perfect world, she'd have kept Poppy sheltered until she was eighteen.

Shawn set the toast down in front of her and rubbed the back of her neck. "What do you want on it?"

"Butter and marmite?"

He grimaced. "Seriously. I thought this was supposed to make you feel better?"

"I like butter and marmite."

"Just don't go asking for a kiss afterwards."

She poked her tongue out at him and got busy with the toast.

They still took separate cars to work, though it wasn't exactly cost effective, and definitely wasn't the best option for the environment. She couldn't risk the questions that would be asked if they showed up together. Besides, she needed to drop

Poppy off at Natasha's for breakfast club, depending on the day, and there was no need for Shawn to get involved with that.

Erica had an appointment that morning with a forensic document examiner. She hoped it would give them some insight into what had been written in blood on the wall, not only what it meant, but also who had written it.

Chapter Seventeen

Her keys still hadn't shown up, and the silly incident with the kettle had unnerved her.

Sadie was going to need to get the lock changed, which was an expense she could have done without. She'd prefer to feel safe, though. It was all over the news and social media that a young couple had been murdered in their flat the other night. It had taken place not far from where Sadie lived. Speculation was that the killer had been known to the couple, so it wasn't as though someone was on a murder spree in Bow, but Sadie still wanted to have the reassurance of a locked door.

Grant had stayed over again, something that had made her feel safer. She hadn't wanted to be alone in the flat. She couldn't keep ignoring the fact she didn't have a key to her own front door, though.

She slipped out of bed while he was still sleeping and called the local locksmith. She told him that she needed the job done as soon as possible, but the timings he gave her weren't ideal.

When she went back upstairs, Grant was awake and sitting up in bed.

"I'm going to need to get a locksmith in to change the lock on the front door," she told him. "It doesn't look like my keys are going to show up anytime soon. Trouble is, they want to arrive between ten and eleven, and I need to be in a meeting then."

"They can't do a different time?" he asked.

"Not today, no. He said they're really busy."

Grant thought for a moment. "I'm happy to wait in for them."

"You are? Haven't you got to work, too?"

"As long as I can use your internet connection, I can do a bit of work remotely. It's not a problem, I promise."

She chewed her lower lip, considering his offer. "That seems like an awful lot to ask of you, especially as we've only just met."

"What difference does it make that we've only just met? Am I only allowed to do something nice for people who've been in my life for a certain amount of time?"

When he phrased it like that, she did feel like she was being silly. She guessed it just seemed like the sort of thing a person would ask of their partner, and they definitely weren't far enough into their relationship to think of things like that. It created a warm glow inside her, though, the thought that she might have someone in her life who could help take the strain of things.

Someone to lean on. She'd never had that.

Still, she remained hesitant. "Are you sure..."

He took both her hands in his. "Sadie, I'm simply offering to open the door for a tradesperson. It's really not that big of a deal."

She exhaled a breath. "Thanks. I know I'm being crazy. It really would be a huge help. I get the impression my boss isn't particularly happy with me at the moment, and he won't be pleased if I tell him I need to take time off."

Grant's brow furrowed. "Why isn't your boss happy with you?"

She shook her head. "No real reason. Honestly, it might just be me being paranoid. I don't know. I'd just prefer not to rock the boat."

"He should be grateful to have you. I know we haven't known each other long, as you've already pointed out, but you're clearly an intelligent, conscientious woman."

Sadie found herself blushing and glanced away. "Oh, I don't know about that."

"Don't put yourself down. But remember, you were put on this planet to *live* not to work. Don't let the job stuff overwhelm everything else."

She smiled at him, grateful. "Thanks, Grant. I needed to hear that. Sometimes it's hard not to get caught up in it all."

She thought about that poor couple who'd been murdered. She knew nothing about their lives, but she'd bet if they'd spent most of their adulthood at the office, they would have wished they'd lived a little, too. Sometimes it was hard not to get caught up in the hamster wheel of working just to pay the bills and forgetting there was more to life.

"It does make me feel better knowing you're here," she told him, "especially after what happened to that couple."

"I won't let anyone hurt you," he reassured her. "It's one good reason to keep me around."

"Well, whoever killed them stabbed the man to death as well as the woman, so there being a man in the flat didn't make any difference. They were about my age, too."

"You don't have to worry, Sadie. No one is going to hurt you."

"I'm not worried," she said, though she was, at least a tiny amount. "Doesn't it make you feel uneasy, though, knowing someone who could do something like that to two innocent people is still out there?"

"People do terrible things to others all the time," he said, "and they get away with it, too. Plenty of things we don't even hear about. Doesn't mean those same people aren't out there, walking around with us just like everyone else."

She shuddered. "That's not making me feel any better."

He put his arm around her shoulders, pulled her closer, and kissed the top of her head. "No one is going to hurt you. I swear it."

She allowed him to comfort her, though she felt like a fraud. It wasn't as though she'd known the murdered couple. It shouldn't really be affecting her like it did. Was it just that she saw herself in the other woman—a similar age, a professional, well put together, at least from the photograph she'd seen.

There was no reason to think she might be the next victim. There were millions of women in London. Besides, speculation was that it had been a crime of passion, most likely an ex-boyfriend or something. Wasn't that the usual statistic, that women were more likely to be killed by a spouse than anyone else?

Why was it the people who were supposed to love you most in the world were also the ones most likely to brutally murder you?

"I'm fine," she said, trying to shake off the black cloud that hovered over her. "I'm just being silly."

"Look, if you're feeling freaked out about sleeping here alone, because the killer is still out there, I'll just stay with you until he's caught, okay?"

She glanced up at him anxiously. "You'd do that?"

"Of course. I'd much rather be here with you than sleeping alone in my own bed, being kept awake by noisy neighbours who think it's okay to party until all hours of the morning. I'd be crazy not to want to."

She touched his jaw, the morning's stubble rough beneath her fingertips. "I'm so thankful I met you, Grant."

"I'm thankful I met you, too. We came into each other's lives at exactly the right time, didn't we?"

"Fate," she said.

He kissed her. "Yes, fate. Some people are just meant to be."

Chapter Eighteen

"I have to admit," the older man said from where he sat in his high-backed chair, "I'm sent a lot of samples of handwriting to analyse, but I'm not sure I've ever been asked to analyse something that's been written in blood."

The forensic document examiner Erica had come to meet was Professor Nigel Reed. He wore a tweed jacket, despite the heat, and had a handlebar moustache which he twirled when he was thinking. He looked like he had stepped right out of an Agatha Christie novel.

"I apologise if that's disturbing for you," Erica said.

"Not at all. It is what it is. I'm happy to help if you think it'll give you an idea of who killed that poor couple."

"It'll certainly help," she encouraged him.

He rubbed the crook of his forefinger across his lips as he studied the image:

You have to stop him.
I'm not strong enough.

"You can get more than five thousand different traits about a person from their handwriting alone," he informed her. "The size of the letters, how close they are, the angles used, and even the indentation of the letters can say a lot about a person. They can even reveal health elements or whether a person is lying."

"I see."

"The problem we have with this sample is that we're only presented with a few words. Obviously, that makes it harder to analyse than if we had an entire handwritten letter, for example. The person who wrote them would also have been using a different angle than they normally would if they were writing with a pen and paper. Also, we have to be aware that they most likely used a gloved hand or finger as a writing implement, blood instead of graphite or ink, and a wall instead of paper. I also normally like to have something to compare the writing to, such as a ransom note, but again, that's not possible."

Erica tamped down her impatience. "Is there anything you *can* tell me, rather than what you can't?"

He cleared his throat. "Yes, of course." He held the photograph of the bloodied writing up to the light. "Do you see these slant changes and the sudden upsurge in height of these letters?"

Erica nodded.

"Well," he continued, "they show recklessness. The trailing end of the letter 'e' shows impulsive emotional reactions. Do you see the long sharp ending to the 'g?' To me that says a level of aggressiveness."

"I don't think anyone is going to argue with you that the killer was aggressive," she said.

"There's one main thing that strikes me about this writing."

"Which is?"

"I believe the person who wrote it is young."

"Young, like 'in their twenties' young?"

He shook his head. "No. The handwriting is childlike." He hesitated. "But I wouldn't go as far as saying it was necessarily done by a child."

"Someone who hasn't been properly schooled, perhaps?" she suggested.

"Or someone who has been sheltered. Who is still living a childlike existence."

"But you also said they're aggressive. Does that normally go hand in hand with being childlike?"

Nigel nodded. "Unfortunately, it can. Let me continue. The 'n' is pointy, which indicates a fast mind, and a closely dotted 'i' tends to come from an organised person."

Erica felt as though she was being delivered a barrage of conflicting information. She'd wanted this meeting to advance the investigation, but instead she was more confused than ever.

"You're saying the writing appears childlike but isn't done by a child, yet is also aggressive, impulsive, organised, and from a sharp mind?"

"Yes, that's exactly what I'm saying."

"Have you ever seen anything like this before?" she asked.

"A note written in blood on a wall? No, I already told you it isn't exactly my preferred medium." He thought for a moment. "But the writing does remind me of something."

"What?"

He twisted his lips. "I can't put my finger on it right now. Can you leave it with me? I'll give you a call when it comes to me."

Erica bit down on her frustration. "Of course, just remember that the sooner we find this person, the less possibility there will be of him hurting anyone else."

She didn't say it, but also the more time that passed where they hadn't tracked down the killer, the colder the leads were going to get. The truth was, they still didn't have anything solid. No CCTV footage, no licence plate numbers, no DNA linked to a potential suspect. All they had was a possible connection to an eighteen-year-old case, and the person convicted for that double murder was still behind bars and so couldn't have committed this more recent crime.

Again, the possibility that Robert Brooks was innocent niggled at her brain. If he was, then the same person might be responsible for the murders.

"I understand that." Nigel frowned, his already lined head folding with wrinkles, his bushy eyebrows becoming one long furry slug. "It'll come to me, I'm sure of it. Do you think this person is likely to do the same thing again?"

"I hope not, but right now, it's impossible to know."

They both stood, and she put out her hand for him to shake.

"You've got my number, haven't you?"

He tapped the business card on the desk that she'd given him. "I certainly do."

Erica thanked him again and left. She headed back to her car.

She needed to go back and study the older case in more detail, try and find something that would say for sure whether they were connected. Forensic science had come on leaps and bounds in the past eighteen years. Maybe there was something that hadn't yielded any results during the initial tests eighteen years ago, but would now.

Could she not only catch a killer but prove a convicted man to be innocent?

Chapter Nineteen

Erica got back in the office shortly before lunch.

"Any development in tracking down the ex-girlfriend? Anna or Emma?" she asked Shawn.

"No, we haven't found anyone by the name in any of Jordon's contacts. His parents didn't know the name either, but there's no reason why he would have told them about every woman he got involved with."

"If she's not in his contacts, it's unlikely that he's been in touch with her recently. I can't imagine a two-year-old breakup suddenly turning this nasty."

"She might be under a different name," he suggested. "Perhaps Jordon was trying to hide the relationship from Tabitha."

Erica let out a sigh. "I don't know. Everyone said how happily married Jordon and Tabitha were. I'm worried we're wasting time by chasing the wrong people."

"If you can point me in the direction of the right person, I'll happily chase them instead," Shawn said.

She gave a groan of frustration. "Yeah, I know. It doesn't feel like we're getting anywhere fast with this case. Anything back from Reggie's phone location check?"

"Yeah, looks like his story is true."

"Or else he just left his phone at home."

The phone on her desk rang, and she excused herself to answer it.

"DI Swift."

"Erica, it's Lee Mattocks."

THE NIGHT PROWLER

Lee was head of CSI for their borough.

"Lee, how are you?"

"Good, but I've got some news for you. We've had a hit on a DNA sample taken from the Moots' crime scene."

She shot a look over to Shawn, trying to tell him from eye contact alone that they'd finally made some progress. "That's excellent news. What have you found?"

"We got a familial hit on DNA that was a sample we had on record from a double murder committed eighteen years ago."

She hadn't been expecting that at all. "Familial DNA?"

"Yes. The DNA found at the two scenes isn't exactly the same. It has a forty-seven point five percent match."

"So, what? Are they siblings, perhaps?"

"With that percentage, it's most likely a father and son."

She let this sink in. "So now we have two unidentified DNA samples?"

An apology laced his tone. "For the moment, yes."

"What was the case from eighteen years ago?" She asked the question, but she already knew the answer.

"The double murder of Beatrice and Jack Gabriel."

"The one Robert Brooks is already serving a life sentence for."

"You already know that?" Lee said, sounding surprised.

"Yes, I've already been to see him. There were several things that mirrored the Gabriel case, and the crime scene photos are almost identical. Now there's this. Are you saying that whoever is responsible for these murders is related to the person who killed the couple back then?"

"No, that's not what I'm saying at all. We don't know that either of those DNA samples even belonged to the killer."

"It's a pretty big coincidence if they don't," she noted.

"Maybe, but we don't have proof of that. It could just be they know the same family and had relatives into their home, and they're connected that way."

He had a point. Maybe the two cases were related because of someone they knew. "Do you think that's likely?" she asked.

"I don't need to tell you that presence of DNA at a crime scene isn't proof alone that it belongs to the killer."

Erica's brain was buzzing. What were they missing?

"If we can prove this more recent DNA belongs to the killer, then it'll also prove Robert Brooks wasn't responsible for killing the Gabriel couple eighteen years ago."

"No, it won't," Lee said down the line. "It's not the same DNA. Maybe if it matched, then yes, I think there would be a good possibility of getting the case reopened, but if it's just a case of a relative of the current killer being in the same place eighteen years ago..." He trailed off. "I don't know, Erica. I don't think that's going to be enough."

"An innocent man might be rotting in prison. He's spent almost eighteen years there. Practically his whole life."

"You don't know he's innocent."

"He's proclaimed his innocence the whole time he's been behind bars."

"The prisons are full of people who insist they're innocent."

"Yeah, I know."

She hated to think that innocent people were wasting away behind bars. When someone was arrested and went through the courts, she wanted to believe that the system was robust enough to ensure mistakes didn't happen. If someone was found guilty, it was because they were actually guilty.

Still, it niggled.

The Gabriel murders hadn't been her case. Who was the detective who'd worked on it? Could she speak to them? Maybe there was something they'd remember that would help. There had to be something. It wasn't a coincidence that a relative's DNA had been found at both crime scenes.

"I'll get everything uploaded," Lee said. "You can check it for yourself."

"Thanks, Lee. If anything else comes up, don't hesitate to contact me."

She ended the call and glanced up to find Shawn watching her. He'd clearly only heard her side of the conversation.

"You're not going to believe this," she told him.

Chapter Twenty

It was easy enough for Erica to find out who'd been the Senior Investigating Officer on the case from eighteen years ago. Learning his name, and actually getting to speak to him, were two different things, however.

DCI Leonard Kerr was retired now.

The lead detective on the case didn't live in the area anymore—in fact, he didn't even live in the country. He'd retired a few years ago and had since moved to Spain, getting in just before the option to retire in the sun was taken away from the rest of the UK.

She started by sending him an email. She hoped it would still be up to date, since Leonard didn't appear to be present on any social media, and she hadn't found a phone number for him. It was early days, and she was sure she'd manage to track him down, but him living in a different country did make things all that much harder.

To her surprise, he replied to her email within the hour, asking for more information and offering his assistance.

He sounded keen to help, and she wondered how easy it was for somebody who'd been this high up in the force to just let everything go and never work again. While she was sure he must be leading a relaxing life now, was his quick response and enthusiasm because he was bored? Maybe he was keen to get his teeth stuck into something again.

She replied back, filling him in on what they'd learned so far about the Moots' case—which wasn't much—and her suspicions about the two cases being linked, together with the finding of the familial DNA at both crime scenes.

Unlike with the first email, she didn't get a response right away, though she assumed he was still online. Was his hesitation because of the historical case she'd mentioned? It must have put a damper on his enthusiasm.

She drummed her fingers against the top of her desk and tried to distract herself with other work. Finally, her email pinged with an incoming message, and she clicked on it. It was short and sweet.

What do you need to know?

She quickly typed back: *Can we do a video call?*

She wanted to be able to see his face when she made the suggestion that the man who'd been locked up for the past eighteen years might not be the right one. She knew it wasn't going to go down well. No one liked to be told they were wrong—especially not on something as important as this. Had Leonard ever had any suspicions that they might be putting away the wrong person? Had they ever considered someone else might be responsible for the murders?

The reply came back: *Okay.*

She sent him a link to a video chat, and within minutes, they were staring at each other through their computer's cameras.

Leonard Kerr had the deep golden tan of someone who spent a lot of time in the sun, and a head of thick white hair. He must be in his sixties by now but could have passed for someone a decade younger. Life on the Costa was clearly doing him good.

"Thank you for taking the time to talk to me," Erica said. "I'll try not to take up too much of your time."

"Not a problem," he replied. "How's life in London?"

"Much the same as when you left it, I'd imagine. How about life in Spain? Are you enjoying retirement?"

He shrugged. "I can't complain. I spend my days on the golf course and my evenings in the local venta, eating tapas and drinking cheap beer."

"Not missing the job then?"

"Nope, not even for a minute. I worked hard all my life to be able to spend my retirement like this. I don't miss the British winters either. Spent Christmas Day having a barbecue last year. It was perfect."

Erica hadn't been abroad in years. She didn't think she'd like to have a hot Christmas, though. It wouldn't feel right. Christmas should be about being huddled around the fire and hoping for snow—even if it never arrived. Having a barbecue in the sun just wouldn't feel Christmassy to her.

"Anyway," he said, sitting back, "enough of the small talk. You wanted to ask me some questions about a case I worked on."

"That's right. The Gabriel case. Do you remember it?"

"Of course. You don't forget a case like that." He shook his head. "The level of violence was like nothing I'd ever seen before. The female victim had been stabbed twenty-three times, and her partner had been stabbed seven times, I think it was. We got the bastard who did it, though. He won't be getting out anytime soon."

"What did you make of him? Robert Brooks, I mean."

"He was sly. Sneaky. One of these men who could charm you, if he wanted, but a devil lay behind the mask."

"I've been to see him in prison," Erica confessed.

"You have? Why?"

"Because of the links to this current case. He came across well, to be honest. He's still maintaining his innocence."

"Don't let him fool you. I know the years have gone by, but there was violence in that man's eyes. He'd sent threatening messages to her, telling her to leave her partner and come back to him, and had said that he wouldn't be able to control himself if she didn't. There was a lot of stuff about life not being worth living if they weren't together. Of course, he made it sound like he was talking about himself, but really he was talking about them. If he couldn't have her, then he didn't want anyone else to either."

"Sending someone messages isn't the same as stabbing them twenty-three times," Erica said.

"It was him," Leonard said with conviction. "His DNA was found on her body. His semen was found inside her because he'd raped her before he killed her. He was even seen outside of her house the same night of the murders. There really wasn't any doubt about his guilt."

"Except that he insisted he's innocent, and unidentified DNA was sampled at the crime scene."

"There's going to be unidentified DNA at every crime scene. It doesn't mean he didn't do it." Leonard took a breath. "Honestly, Detective, if you could have seen the state of those bodies, the number of times he'd plunged the knife in and out of them, well, they were left like minced meat, parts of them."

"I think I know exactly what you mean. This recent case is very similar. If I sent you a couple of photographs, could you tell me your thoughts? Tell me if it looks like it was done by the same perpetrator?"

He sat back and folded his arms. "How can it be done by the same perpetrator when he's currently behind bars?"

"I'm not sure. But now we have unidentified DNA at a second crime scene, eighteen years later, that has a forty-seven point five percent match to the DNA found at the Gabriel scene. Surely that's got to raise some doubt?"

The blue of his eyes hardened to glacial ice. "You're not suggesting we got the wrong man eighteen years ago?"

"I'm not suggesting anything. I'm simply asking for your thoughts." She was careful with her words, not wanting to alienate him. He had been the SIO on the case, and while she was sure there were others who'd worked on it, she wanted to get his opinion. "Maybe we're looking at a copycat killing, or there might have been more than one person involved. We're considering that possibility for the Moots' case, because of what was written on the wall. I wouldn't be doing my job right if I didn't dig into these things."

He pressed his lips together and considered what she'd said. "A second perpetrator? It wasn't something we considered at the time, but it is a possibility. Why start again, though, eighteen years later?" He scrubbed his hand over his mouth. "Why would someone else have been involved? It was a crime of passion? It doesn't make sense."

She released a breath. "Not much about this case is making sense right now. It would seem the killer just let themselves into the flat, said hello to the dog, who then allowed itself to be shut outside, and then murdered two people without them ever trying to escape or even scream for help. No one saw or heard anything. We're talking about this happening in a built-up area with neighbours all around. It's like this person was a ghost."

"A ghost who likes murdering people and writing on the wall in their blood."

"And likes dogs," she added. "The writing on the wall is the one thing that separates this case from the one you worked on eighteen years ago. No one wrote anything then, did they?"

"No. That definitely would have gone down in the files." He paused and reached for the keyboard of his laptop, switching between screens.

Erica watched his eyes flick back and forth as he took in the photographs she had emailed him. She remained silent, giving him time to process what he was seeing. She knew he wouldn't want to admit there was a possibility whoever had stabbed the Moots had also stabbed the Gabriels, but she hoped he'd retained enough professionalism to tell her what he really thought, rather than trying to protect his own ego.

Eventually, he sat back again. "I don't know what to tell you. Yes, it could be the same perp, but then again, it might not be. It's impossible to tell."

She wanted to reach through the screen and grab him, and shout in his face that it wasn't impossible to tell, that the stab wounds had a certain pattern to them, but she could already tell that she'd lost him.

He wasn't going to admit that he might be wrong.

"Thank you for your time," she said. "I can see I'm keeping you from your golf."

Despite herself, she couldn't help biting out those final words. It was easy for him to just brush this off. He wasn't the one staring into the grief-stricken faces of the families and promising them that she'd find justice for their loved ones. He also wasn't the one who'd met with a potentially innocent man and seen what eighteen years behind bars had done to him.

"If I think of anything that might be of help," Leonard said, "I'll let you know."

"You have my number now. I'd appreciate it if you did."

Maybe he would let it linger on his mind, trouble him as he stood at the fourth hole and tried to take a swing. Maybe he'd close his eyes at night and the pictures of the bodies would appear on the backs of his eyelids, insisting he pay attention.

No matter what the retired detective had said, Erica hadn't changed her mind. If anything, the conversation had only solidified her belief that the two cases were connected, and the man currently behind bars may well be innocent.

Chapter Twenty-One

Liam didn't feel good. His stomach churned and swirled, and he didn't want to sit still. It was as though his veins were filled with a million buzzing insects, making him more and more uncomfortable. He wanted to stand up and run around, pound his fists into the walls, shout and scream at the top of his lungs. But he couldn't. Dad would never put up with such a display of uncontrolled behaviour.

His father wouldn't shout at him or hit him. In a way, Liam wished he would. That would be easier to handle. Bruises faded, and shouting gave him the opportunity to shout back. No, instead, his father fell silent. The disappointment radiating from him without him ever needing to say a word. And then he would tell Liam to go to his room, which Liam would do, and his father would shut the door behind him and lock it.

How long he'd be left in there alone was really dependent on how angry his father was. Sometimes, Liam would get lucky, and he'd have a glass of water or even a protein bar left over from the previous day, so he'd at least have some sustenance, but more often than not, he'd be locked in the room with nothing.

The first few hours were always fine. He might be a little thirsty or hungry, but he was used to that. Often, he'd take himself to bed and sleep through much of it. But when he woke, that was when the real hunger and thirst kicked in.

Liam got to his feet and went to the door. "Dad? Can I come out now?"

He could hear his father moving around in the rest of the house. He was talking, though Liam knew Dad must be just talking to himself. They'd never had someone else in the house, not even for a visit.

Liam pressed his ear to the door and listened to his father's words.

"Do you see what these stupid bitches are doing now. Bringing about some lawsuit because they think a man in power took advantage of them. Look at them, and then look at him. Yeah, he might have had plenty of sway in the business, but if they slept with him to get ahead, that was their choice. Don't tell me they didn't know exactly what they were doing. He probably made their careers, and then they turn around twenty years later and cry about it. They should be thanking him, not trying to sue him. But then that's what they're all about, isn't it. The money. They're getting older, and their beauty is fading, and they have to figure out what they can do for the cash now. No one wants to touch their dried-up pussies anymore, so they turn around and scream rape and try to milk more out of the poor guy that way."

"Dad?" Liam said again.

His father's voice came louder, his footsteps stopping right outside Liam's door.

"Did you hear me, boy? Do you not see what they're doing? Bunch of whores and sluts, and they're getting away with it. All these media people, too, supporting them, making out that these women are the victims, when it's the man who is being treated like a criminal. It's disgusting. Someone needs to teach these bitches a lesson."

Liam had been on the computer and read through the comments on the sites his father liked him to go on. His dad wasn't the only one who felt that way. Plenty of comments included both rape and death threats against the women.

His dad continued his rant. "One day, you're going to have to take up the baton on this fight, do you understand that? I won't be strong enough, and the community needs men like us out there, not just typing messages on the internet but actually doing something."

"I know, Dad." Liam hoped that if he said what his father wanted to hear, then he might let him out, or at least bring him something nice to eat.

"That's why I'm teaching you everything now. It's important. The most important thing you'll ever do as a man."

Liam didn't want to let his dad down.

Chapter Twenty-Two

Erica called a briefing and filled the rest of her team in on what she'd learned.

The day was already passing in a blur. She hadn't found time to eat lunch yet and was feeling a little lightheaded. She promised herself that she'd grab something just as soon as she'd made sure her team were heading in the right direction.

"How has everyone else been getting on?" she asked her team.

Jon started first. "I'm still working on pinning down all Tabitha's and Jordon's final movements leading up to their murders. So far, nothing unusual has come up. They both seem to follow a fairly regular routine of going to work, doing grocery shopping, and coming home again, always around the same sort of time. They had a meal out two nights before they were killed, so I've requested CCTV from the restaurant. They caught a taxi home, and again, we're tracking down the driver. I don't know if that's going to be of any help, but maybe the driver saw someone hanging around outside the flat."

"Good thinking," Erica told him. "I know this isn't easy, but we need to find a connection between the Gabriel case and the Moots. It's been eighteen years, but familial DNA was found in both the crime scenes, so there must be a connection. We've always thought the Moots' killer might be someone they know, so what if the Moots and the Gabriels have a shared family friend?" She shook her head. "There has to be something."

Hannah spoke up. "I don't know if this is something we should be concerned about, but I came across some chatter online."

More and more recently, Erica found that investigation work involved being online. While actual crime scenes and forensics would always be important, some people lived their whole lives online. It also gave them the opportunity to do and say things they'd never dream of doing in real life. Online was where they let the true version of themselves come out, no fears of repercussion when they said what they really thought.

"What's it saying?" she asked.

"Some people are saying that the murders are incel killings, and they're encouraging others to do the same."

Erica frowned. "Incels? Involuntarily celibate men. Is that right?"

"That's right. They're not a pleasant group."

Erica divided this into two parts. "First of all, why would they be incel killings? I thought incels only hated women? It was a couple who was killed."

"I thought the same, but I did a little digging. These men don't only hate the women. They also hate the men who get to sleep with women when they don't. They have names for them both. The women are known as Stacys and the men are called Chads."

Erica rolled her eyes. "Wow, that's a full-on way of saying my dick is too small."

"I know, right. They basically think the whole genetic thing has been rigged against them since birth. That they're never going to get a woman because they don't look like 'Chads.'"

"Or maybe it's just because they're arseholes?" Erica suggested.

Hannah nodded. "Exactly, but they'd rather blame the fact they don't look like models. They believe women are completely superficial, that they are only interested in appearance and money, and if you're someone who has neither, then you're never going to get laid."

Erica sniffed. "Interesting how they call women superficial, but they're the ones who are only interested in women because they want to have sex with them."

"For the most part, they hate women. They have zero respect for women. They don't want a relationship with them. They only want their bodies, and they're pissed off that women don't want them in return."

"Wonder why, when they sound like such a catch."

"From what I can tell, they very rarely ask themselves if it might be a problem with their personality rather than the way they look. As though women would want to get involved with someone who is so full of hate."

Erica moved on to the second part. "You said they were encouraging others to commit more murders?"

Hannah got to her feet and handed the printouts to Erica. "These are some of the conversations going on. Read them for yourself."

Erica let her gaze run across the page. With each line she read, a heavy sense of dismay built inside her. Was this really the world her daughter was growing up in? Where someone could hate a person simply because they didn't get what they wanted?

<Whoever killed the Stacy and Chad needs to go into some kind of hall of fame. Taking both of them out at the same time—what a legend.>

<I heard he fucked her first, too. Finally got the whore to spread her legs for one of us.>

<I hope he made the Chad watch before he stabbed him to death.>

<This is an uprising. Let this inspire you!>

<If anyone is thinking of topping themselves anytime soon, be a hero and take another Stacy and Chad down with you.>

<They got what they deserved.>

Erica shook her head in disgust. "What's the chance of there actually being a connection? Or is this just a bunch of butt-hurt idiots trying to make themselves seem like the big man?"

Hannah shrugged. "None of them have said anything that they wouldn't have got from the news or social media reports."

"So they're most likely just speculating and using the murders as an excuse to stir up their fellow incels." Erica turned and pinned the printout onto the incident board. She thought it was unlikely the two murders were connected to this group, but that didn't mean there wouldn't be some fallout from it. "What's the chances of someone actually taking this seriously, though? I'd hate for there to be another murder because someone spurred on one of these arseholes."

"I can try and get the chat taken down," Hannah said, "but you know what it's like. You shut down one and they just pop up somewhere else."

"That's the trouble with the internet. No real regulation."

They'd worked on a case recently where murders were being live-streamed, and there was still nothing they could do to get them taken down. There was still footage available online even now, months later, and there probably always would be. Once something was out there, it was impossible to completely pull back again.

"Let's monitor it, make sure nothing evolves from it."

When a suggestion was put in the mind of an angry young man who thought the world was out to get him, he didn't always confide in other people about what he planned to do.

Were they about to get a flurry of copycat killings happening across London? The possibility sickened her. The victims were just normal people, living their lives. They didn't deserve to die simply because some man with a complex decided they were the enemy.

She thought to her and Shawn's new relationship. Would someone christen them as a Stacy and Chad? She highly doubted it—she was too old, for a start. But she had to admit that it made her thankful that their relationship was under wraps.

The hatred online troubled her, however.

"Shawn," she said, "think you can give Jasmin a call, see if she can dig into things any further?"

"Absolutely," he replied.

Chapter Twenty-Three

Sadie had been messaging on and off with Grant all day, making sure her boss didn't notice that she was distracted from her work.

The locksmith had arrived and replaced her lock, which was a relief, so now she had a new set of keys—or at least Grant did. She hadn't seen him yet to take them from him.

She told him it was fine for him to leave them in the house and go to work, but then she realised he had her only back door key as well. If he left and locked up the house, she'd be locked back out again.

She really needed to get smarter about her home security.

In the end, though, he'd decided it was probably just easier for him to work from her place, and then he'd be there when she got back from work.

Now it was home time, and it was strange coming back to the flat, knowing someone was there waiting for her. She wondered how Monty had felt about having company all day. He'd probably loved it. She also hoped she hadn't put Grant out too much. He'd done her a favour, and she didn't want him to think she was taking advantage.

She parked the car and then used the rear entrance, since she still didn't have a front door key.

She opened the back door, which wasn't locked, to be hit with the delicious smell of something meaty cooking.

"Hi, honey, I'm home," she called out in a sing-song voice, hoping he'd take it in the tongue-in-cheek way it was meant.

"Hi." He appeared in the kitchen doorway, a glass of red wine in his hand. "I got dinner on. I hope you don't mind?"

"Mind? Coming home to a cooked meal? Are you crazy? Why would I mind?"

He set down the wine glass, caught her around the waist, and kissed her. "I've missed you all day."

"I've missed you, too. Don't feel you have to stay, though. I've monopolised you enough."

"I want to stay..." He hesitated. "But I'll go if you'd prefer to be on your own."

At least she knew he wasn't married. There was no way he could be spending this much time at her place if he was.

They ate the slow-cooked lamb shanks he'd made, the meat melting on her tongue, and shared the rest of the bottle of red wine.

"It all went okay with the locksmith then?" she asked.

"Yes, though I had a work call when he was here, so I kind of just left him to it. I hope that's all right."

"Of course." She grinned. "I didn't expect you to babysit him. I appreciate that you were here."

He pointed his knife at her. "Don't let me forget to give you your new keys."

"Thanks. It'll be good to be able to use my front door again."

After they'd eaten, she insisted on doing the washing up and told him to go and sit down. When she was done, she made them both a cup of tea and carried them into the living room.

Grant was bent over her desk. One of the drawers was open, and he was rifling through it. He seemed so focused on his task that he hadn't even noticed her entering the room.

Something about his stance sent ripples of worry through her. It was furtive, like he was trying to work quickly. She'd never specifically told him not to go through her belongings—she hadn't thought such an instruction was necessary—but now he was doing it, it felt weird. She had a lot of paperwork in her desk. All her credit card bills, her contracts for work, the occasional personal letter or card she'd decided to keep. Him digging through them all was an invasion of privacy.

"Looking for something?" she asked, keeping her tone light.

She set the two mugs down on the coffee table.

He jolted upright, and then shoved the drawer shut, and spun to face her. "Just trying to find a pen."

"A pen? What do you need a pen for?"

That easy, comfortable smile was back on his face. "Maybe I wanted to write you a love note. A poem, perhaps."

She arched an eyebrow. "You wanted to write me a poem?"

"It's something you haven't learnt about me yet." He shrugged. "That's okay. I guess there's still a lot we don't know about each other. This is the fun part, isn't it, discovering all those little things about the other person that we never guessed might lie beneath the surface."

"And yours is that you like to write poetry."

His brow tugged down slightly. "Why is that so unbelievable?"

She gave a small laugh. "Honestly, I'm not sure. You just didn't strike me as someone who would like poetry. I didn't even know if you read poetry, never mind write it yourself. Do you have anything published?"

"No, I'm not interested in publishing. I just like to write for myself. It's cathartic." He stepped forwards and wrapped his arm around her waist, pulling her into him. "And now I have my very own muse."

She wasn't sure how she felt about being someone's muse. It definitely wasn't something she'd ever considered before.

"So, did you find one?" she asked.

"Find what?"

"A pen? And do you have some paper? I think I'd rather like to read a poem someone has written about me."

He chuckled. "No, I didn't, and you can't just demand for it to be written. I have to be inspired."

Hadn't he just said that she was the one inspiring him? Stupidly, she was disappointed, but then maybe he was right, and it wasn't something a person could just churn out on demand. She'd never been a particularly creative person. She liked numbers, and facts and figures. She liked it when the answer to a question wasn't open to interpretation. It was either right or wrong. She hadn't been bad at English at school, but it definitely hadn't been her favourite subject either. She'd preferred maths and science.

She stood on her tiptoes to place a kiss on his mouth. "I'll wait as long as I need to. I bet I'll enjoy reading it all the more if I have to wait."

"Yes, the anticipation will make it all the sweeter."

He kissed her back, and her heart swelled. She couldn't believe how lucky she was to have found this man. She'd honestly started to believe this kind of relationship was never going to happen for her. There had been so many arseholes in her life that a part of her had thought all men were going to be like that. She'd watched her friends meet their partners, get married, and settle down, and they always seemed happy—other than the occasional moan that their other half wasn't pulling his weight with the housework or was going out too often with his friends—but deep down she'd wondered if it was all just an act.

Now she'd met Grant and already she was struggling to picture her life without him in it. She didn't want to get ahead of herself, but maybe there was a chance they'd be able to build a life together.

That he'd been going through her stuff irked her, but she told herself that she must be overreacting. After all, he'd been alone in the flat all day. If he wanted to go through her private papers for some reason, why would he wait until she was home?

Sadie knew she needed to trust people more, but sometimes it wasn't easy to let a stranger into your life.

Chapter Twenty-Four

Erica and Shawn had been invited to dinner over at the Webbs' house.

"Sorry we're late." Erica pushed a bottle of wine into Jasmin's hands. "Work ran over."

"You're just on time, actually," Jas said. "Mum's dishing up now."

"Something smells incredible," Shawn said, lifting his nose to the air.

"It's Mum's jerk chicken, rice, and beans."

"Is it spicy?" Poppy asked.

Jasmin laughed. "Everything my mother cooks is spicy. Do you think you'll be okay with eating it?"

Poppy nodded. "I can do spice."

"You're a tough girl, huh?" Jasmin teased.

"My mum didn't raise me to be a wimp."

Erica laughed and smoothed down Poppy's hair. "No, I certainly didn't. Us girls have to be tough."

"But with a soft centre," Jas added.

Over the past few months, Erica had got to know Shawn's cousin a lot better. This wasn't the first time they'd been over for dinner at Jasmin's mother's house. Gloria was a joy to be around, and her food was incredible.

They were all funnelled into the kitchen, where they said their hellos to Gloria who stood at the oven, stirring food in a pot.

"Sit, sit," she told them.

The table was already set. They'd all be crammed around it, but that didn't matter. It was the company and good food that counted.

"Is there anything I can do to help?" Erica offered.

Gloria shook her head. "Not at all. You've been at work all day. Let me take some of the load."

Gloria helped with a charity every Sunday called the Good Food Fight, where they made hot meals for the homeless or even simply those who were struggling at the moment, and handed the bags out to anyone who might need it, no questions asked. Knowing Gloria's cooking, it was probably restaurant quality meals made on a budget. Sometimes it was the only hot meal these people got each week. She was one of those selfless souls who gave to their community. The individuals at the heart of it. London would be a far crueller, colder place without people like her.

Shawn opened the wine for the adults and a can of lemonade for Poppy, and Gloria bustled around them, dishing up plates of food and setting them on the table.

Poppy put one bite of chicken into her mouth and turned around to Erica.

"Why doesn't your chicken ever taste like this, Mum?"

Gloria playfully tapped the girl around the head. "Don't be rude to your mother."

"No, she's right," Erica said. "My chicken doesn't taste like this. In fact, none of my food ever tastes this good. I'm afraid I'm not much of a whizz in the kitchen."

Gloria flapped her hand. "Well, you've got more important things to be doing, haven't you? Like catching criminals."

"I try," she replied with a smile.

After they'd eaten and helped to clear up, Erica left Poppy with Gloria. While Gloria wasn't exactly old enough to be of a grandma age, Erica liked seeing Poppy interact with her. She'd never had a grandmother figure in her life.

Poppy was showing Gloria a game she was playing on her phone and then letting Gloria have a go. Lots of shrieks of laughter came from the pair, their heads buried close together.

"You wanted to talk to me about something?" Jasmin asked, half closing the door to give them some privacy.

Erica was grateful to her for that. She didn't want Poppy to hear what was being said. While she knew she wasn't going to be able to protect her daughter from the evils of the world forever, she wanted to keep her sheltered as best she could.

Erica launched right in. "I'm sure you've heard about the murder of that couple in Bow."

"Of course. It's been all over the news and social media. Have you got any leads?"

"Nothing substantial yet. But what we do have is a tenuous link to the incel movement—if I can even call it a 'movement.'"

Jasmin's brown eyes narrowed. "Incels? Aren't they men who hate women?"

"Pretty much," Shawn said. "They're a pretty pathetic group of people. They blame women for the fact no one wants to sleep with them."

Erica drew a breath in through her nose. "It goes a bit deeper than that. They believe that genetics is rigged against them and that women are so shallow that they're not interested in someone who doesn't have a square jaw or is six feet tall."

"Or maybe they're just arseholes and women can tell that," Jas said.

Shawn grinned at her. "You'd think, wouldn't you?"

Jasmin thought of something. "But hang on, I thought it was a couple who was murdered, not just a woman."

"That's right," Erica said. "They hate men as well. Anyone who got lucky in the genetic lottery can be a target. They hate that those people get to be happy together while they're alone."

"And still a virgin?" Jasmin commented.

"Some of them are, yes. The problem is that it's easy to ridicule them, because they're blaming others for their lack of romantic success and their loneliness, but some of them can be very dangerous. There are many cases of these young men turning violent."

"And you think that's what happened with the Bow case?"

"Honestly, we're unsure right now, and it's unlikely, but the murders have been picked up by the incel community, and they're using it as an excuse to encourage others to do the same. Have you seen a photograph of the couple who were killed? They were both attractive, and I guess the incels are happy to have two fewer beautiful people in the world."

"Bastards," Jasmin muttered.

"Exactly," Erica agreed.

Jas sat back. "So what can I do to help?"

"Our resources are stretched to breaking point. Would you be able to keep an eye on the online forums where the murders are being mentioned, see if anything gets posted that seems to have any insider knowledge into the case? Can you also keep an eye out on anyone who might be looking like they're considering doing the same to someone else. We've seen a lot of calls to incite violence come off the back of the Moots' murders."

"And if I see something?"

"Would you be able to narrow down where the person is posting from? If they're local?"

Jasmin nodded. "It would really depend on what kind of encryption they're using, if any, but I can certainly try."

"We'd appreciate that. It might be that there's no connection to what happened, and these sick fucks are just getting off on it, but if there is one, we want to know."

"Understood."

Gloria called from the other room, "Anyone ready for some pudding?"

Erica put her hand over her stomach and groaned. "I'm not sure I've got space."

Jasmin raised her eyebrows. "This is my mum's treacle sponge. Trust me, you're going to want to make space."

Chapter Twenty-Five

"Let's call in sick," Grant suggested.

Sadie lay in bed with her head pillowed on Grant's bicep. He'd stayed over again last night. Neither of them had wanted him to go home. She'd been fighting with herself about getting up and jumping in the shower to get ready for work, though she really didn't want to.

She raised her head slightly to look at him. "What?"

"I don't want to have to spend all day without you. We should pull a sickie and spend all day in bed."

As tantalising as that sounded, she couldn't, and she let out a groan. "I have work to do. I have meetings. I can't just call in sick."

He pulled her in closer and kissed her. "Someone must be able to cover for you. What would happen if you actually *were* sick? You wouldn't be expected to still go to meetings, would you?"

She hesitated. "No...I suppose not."

He grinned. "So let's stay home then."

"I'll have to call in. My boss might even expect me to do some video calls."

"That's okay. I'm sure I can let you go for long enough to do that. Just no longer, okay? I want you all to myself. I don't like sharing."

As well as the thought of calling in sick, something else bothered her. He was talking about staying here again, but didn't he need to go home sometime? To get a change of clothes or a toothbrush—though she'd given him a new one from a packet in the bathroom cabinet? Was there a reason he didn't want to go back to his flat?

Sadie bit on her lower lip and forced herself to speak up. "When will I get to see your place? We're at mine all the time."

"Your flat is far nicer than mine."

She shrugged. "That doesn't mean I don't want to see where you live. Besides, something being nicer is only a matter of opinion. I'm sure your home is fine."

Her stomach knotted. Why was he making excuses? Had her colleague been right? Perhaps he was trying to hide something, like he was married or in a relationship, and that was why he didn't want her coming back to his? But if this was just a fling—an affair—why love bomb her like this? If he was already in a relationship, then this wasn't going to go anywhere. Why bother making her feel as though she was the only one in the world for him.

He must have sensed something was wrong. "What is it?"

She decided there was no point in lying. "It bothers me that you won't allow me to see where you live. It makes me worry that you're hiding a part of your life from me, like a part of your life that contains a girlfriend or even a wife."

He stared at her and then burst out laughing. "You really think I'd be here with you, like this, if I had someone else?"

"I don't know. That's why I'm asking." She noted that he hadn't really answered the question.

"You should know me better than that."

"But I don't know you, do I? It's been less than a week since we met. That's nothing. And I don't really know anything about you."

"I'll tell you whatever you want to know. It might have only been a matter of days, but that doesn't change how I feel about you. When you meet the right person, you just know. That's how I feel about you, Sadie, and I really hope you feel the same way."

He searched her eyes beseechingly, and she could feel herself falling. Wasn't this what she'd been wanting for so long? She'd so badly wanted somebody she could call her own, yet now here was a gorgeous, attentive, loving man, and she was pushing him away. It was no wonder she was so lonely all the time if this was how she reacted to somebody offering their heart. She couldn't decide if she was being overly cautious or if she was just being sensible. Wasn't this simply what happened when you fell in love with someone? You wanted to be with them all the time. Yet the intensity of his feelings seemed a little too much. It made her want to pull away. But what if by pulling away she ruined everything?

He squeezed her hand. "If you really want to see my flat, then of course I'll show it to you. I just didn't want you to think badly of me in any way."

Now she was anxious for another reason. What the hell was so wrong with his place that she'd think badly of him for it?

She gave a nervous laugh. "It can't be that bad."

He sighed. "You were right when you suspected I didn't live alone."

Her stomach dropped like she was in a plane and they'd hit a patch of turbulence. "Oh."

"Not like that! I have flatmates. I'm embarrassed that at my age, I can't even afford my own place."

She exhaled in relief. "Oh, that's okay. I mean, these are London prices, right? It's crazy expensive to rent or buy."

"I know, but I'm thirty-seven years old. I shouldn't still have flatmates. I'd always imagined I'd have my own place by this age," he shot her a look, "maybe even be married by now, have a couple of kids running around."

"You want children?"

"God, yes, absolutely. I'm not saying right this minute, but I definitely see a family in my future. I can't imagine growing old and grey and not leaving some kind of legacy behind. What about you? Can you see yourself having children one day?"

Her heart sang. "Definitely. I've always wanted a family. It feels like that's the reason I was put on the earth."

They grinned at each other.

"So, you'll call in sick then?" he reminded her. "We can spend the day here?"

"Yeah, okay."

She ignored the twist of unease in her gut that told her this was a bad idea, that she had people depending on her, and she was only going to end up stressed out when she fell behind with her work. She wanted to spend more time with him. How often did these kinds of situations happen? She was allowed to be selfish just this once, wasn't she?

Sadie found her phone and left the bedroom so she could have some privacy. If she needed to put on an act, she couldn't have Grant distracting her.

She called her boss, Tony, and put on a croaky voice.

"I'm sorry, but I think I ate something bad last night. Must have been the prawn curry. I've been up all night, and it's not been pretty. I'm not going to make it in today."

"You're joking, Sadie," Tony said down the line. "Don't you have a representative from the Patterson account coming in for a meeting today?"

She was great at her job. She'd been hoping for a promotion sometime soon and maybe she'd even be able to make partner in the future. She worked hard. The clients liked her and trusted her. Now she felt as though she was letting everyone down.

She almost forgot to put on her poorly voice. "I'm sure someone else can speak to them, or else we can reschedule. I'm really not well, Tony. You honestly wouldn't want me representing the firm today. I'd be likely to send the Patterson account running to our nearest competitor."

It was strange how she was almost starting to believe her own lie. She wasn't sick at all, but then when was the last time she'd called in sick? It had been so long ago that she couldn't even remember the date. Surely her boss shouldn't be angry with her for calling in this once? It wasn't as though she did it every day.

"Fine," he said. "I'll put Yvonne on it, but she might need to contact you to check up on some details."

"I'll keep my phone on. I promise."

She ended the call and returned to the bedroom.

Grant was still sitting in bed, and she wondered why he hadn't needed to make an awkward phone call. He clearly had far more flexible hours than she did.

"You okay?" he asked.

"Yeah. My boss just wasn't happy about me calling in sick."

"You can't help being sick."

She rolled her eyes. "Maybe not, but I'm not actually ill, am I? I don't have food poisoning."

"He didn't know that."

She sighed. "Yeah, I know. That did kind of piss me off. It's not like I call in sick all the time."

"You know what they say about work. Don't kill yourself trying to please a boss who would replace you in a second."

Sadie let this sink in. Was she really so replaceable? She hadn't thought so until this moment. She'd always thought she had a good relationship with her clients, and that wasn't something someone else could just sweep in and take over. But he was right in that it could happen. If they needed to have redundancies, as one of the younger members of staff, she would probably be one of the first to go. If she put all of her time and energy into work at the expense of her personal life, what would she have if she did lose her job?

"It doesn't matter," she said. "Besides, I can't take it back, so I might as well make the most of today, right?"

He pulled her down into his arms. "Exactly."

Chapter Twenty-Six

Erica felt like she must be coming down with a bug. Despite being nauseated and lightheaded, she forced herself into work. Almost a week had passed since the Moots' murders, and they had more questions than answers.

They hadn't found any connection between the Moots and the Gabriels, and had no idea who either DNA sample belonged to.

Before she'd even managed to make herself coffee, DCI Gibbs called her into his office.

"It's been almost a week since the murders, Erica," he said. "We need to make some progress on this."

"We've made progress—"

He held up his hand to stop her. "Not enough. A tenuous link between two DNA samples and an eighteen-year-old case is not helping to narrow things down."

"It's not a tenuous link," she argued. "It's a solid one, and I think it's going to prove that Robert Brooks shouldn't be behind bars."

"Don't get sidetracked by Robert Brooks. We need to find out who's responsible for this case, not one that happened eighteen years ago."

"I believe that if we figure out one, it'll lead us to the other. Right now, I believe there might be two perpetrators, and they're related. Most likely a father and son, and they could have been known to both couples."

"We need more. The press are having a field day with us, saying we're not up to the job."

"I'm aware of that, sir. I promise we're doing everything we can."

"Do more," he insisted.

Erica left his office, frustrated and annoyed. She didn't like getting chewed out by her boss.

Shawn caught her attention. "I've been going back over the case file and noticed an item that was found in Tabitha Moots' purse. It might be nothing, but she had a receipt for a new set of keys to be cut."

Erica considered this. "Did she have a set cut for someone? Is the new set in the house somewhere?"

"We found two sets of keys, one belonging to Tabitha, and the other to Jordon, we assume. They both had their own vehicles so had different car keys on the fobs. Looking at the shine on the house key on Tabitha's set, I'd say hers is the new key."

"Did she lose her set, or was a set stolen?"

"Unsure, but we've been wondering how the killer got into the flat. Had they stolen her keys?"

"It makes sense," Erica said. "If they had a key, they simply let themselves in, put the dog in the back garden, murdered both victims, and let themselves out again." She thought for a moment. "We need to find out more about exactly where Tabitha lost her keys and when. Did she actually lose them, or did someone steal them from her bag?"

He nodded. "I'll go back through her social media and see if she's posted anything about losing her keys."

"Good idea. If we can find out when and where it happened, we might be able to track down some CCTV and get whoever took them on camera."

It sounded like exactly the sort of solid lead they needed.

Shawn lowered his voice and jerked his chin towards Gibbs' office door. "Everything go okay in there?"

"Yeah, he was just blowing off steam. He's frustrated we don't have anyone behind bars yet."

"Aren't we all?"

Erica returned to her desk and checked her email. She'd wondered if she might have heard from Leonard Kerr—having some time to think on things might have jogged his memory, or perhaps his conscience, but it didn't look that way.

She'd barely got through the first few emails when Shawn interrupted her again.

"Found something. She posted this three weeks before her murder."

<Having such a shit day. Didn't sleep well and then I somehow managed to lose my house keys so I couldn't get into the flat. Thank you to my hubbie, Jordon, for saving the day and letting me in. Going to need to get a new key cut now.>

"If we're on the right track," he carried on, "it means whoever did this planned a long way ahead."

"We know they planned this. They went to the flat with gloves and even condoms. This was carefully thought out. It doesn't surprise me at all that they might have been planning it for a month or more. Maybe they even got pleasure in the planning. Enjoyed the anticipation of it all." Erica reread the Facebook post. "There's no mention about the location where she thinks the keys were lost or taken. Without that, we can't get CCTV."

"Maybe she spoke to the person she got the key cut with? Complained to them about losing the key in a certain place."

"It's certainly worth asking the question. What's the name of the shop on the receipt?

He showed it to her. "It's the local one for the area."

Erica knew it. The place was local to her, too. She'd often popped in there to get new insoles for her shoes or even have a key cut herself. She didn't know if they'd keep CCTV going back a month, but it was worth trying. Someone might have been following Tabitha when she got the key cut. If there was a possibility the killer wasn't known to the couple, then they would have needed to learn where Tabitha lived, and following her home might have been one way of doing that.

Chapter Twenty-Seven

Happy to have an excuse to get out of the office and get some fresh air, Erica drove to the shop where Tabitha had got her key cut. The place didn't only do key-cutting—they offered a variety of services, including mending shoes, dry-cleaning, and watch repairs.

It was quiet today, only a couple of people browsing. One person sat on a chair near the counter, waiting, perhaps, for their dry-cleaning to be ready.

She spotted a man in his thirties wearing a branded T-shirt working behind the counter and approached him.

"Hello," he said, "can I help you?"

He didn't seem particularly interested in her. He was more focused on rearranging a board containing multiple different style of keys on the back wall.

She slid her ID across the counter. "My name is DI Swift. Can I take a minute of your time?"

He glanced over his shoulder and frowned. "Oh, sure." He brushed his palms on the front of his trousers and faced her fully. "What can I do for you?"

"I'm investigating the murder of two people that happened last week, and I have reason to believe one of the victims used this shop to have her house key cut."

"Okay," he said, still waiting for the question.

"According to the receipt we found, it was done on the twenty-ninth of May, at two twenty-six p.m. It was a Monday. Would you have been working then?"

"I work most weekdays. I was probably here. But we get a lot of customers. I'm not going to remember something about someone who came in over a month ago."

"Can you just take a look at this picture? Is there any chance you recognise her?"

She slid a photograph of Tabitha onto the counter. He glanced down at it, squinting slightly. She studied his expression as he bent over the photo. Was there even a hint of recognition in his eyes?

"No, I'm sorry. I really don't recognise her."

The picture had been plastered all over the news and social media the moment they'd released the victims' names to the press. She was surprised he hadn't recognised her from there, but then maybe he was one of those people who didn't do social media or the news.

"You're sure?" she checked.

"Sorry. Like I said, we get a lot of people coming through here, and a month is a long time ago. I probably wasn't even paying attention, if it was even me who served her. There are several other employees."

"Do you have CCTV footage?"

She glanced up at the cameras in the corner. They were angled down to this exact spot. She was pretty sure she was being recorded right now. If Tabitha had come in here to get her key cut, she'd have been filmed. Maybe someone was watching her at the time? A lurker they might recognise.

He followed her line of sight. "Yeah, but not from a month ago. I think it gets wiped once a week."

She hadn't really been sure what she was going to get from the visit here anyway. It had seemed like something to follow up on, but unless someone remembered Tabitha, or they got her on CCTV, it was a dead end.

She gave him her business card. "If you do remember her, will you give me a call?"

At the back of the store, Erica caught sight of another employee slipping out the back of the shop.

"Who is that?" she asked. "Might they have been here the day Tabitha came in?"

"Possibly, though he only works part time. Between you and me, I doubt he'd remember. He's not the sharpest tool in the box."

She remained in place, her gaze locked on the door where the other man had vanished. "What's the other employee's name?"

He glanced over his shoulder, "Oh, that's Coulter."

"Do you have a rota, so I can check who'd have been on when she came in?"

"Yeah, but it changes each week. I don't know if any copies are kept, but I can find out for you."

"Thanks, I appreciate it."

Chapter Twenty-Eight

Dad had left him alone with the laptop.

It was a huge responsibility. He'd been told that he needed to reply to their comrades online. Let them know they're not alone.

Liam was used to this. He often posed as his father online, though normally it was with Dad sitting beside him. It was what his dad wanted—for him to experience the community, the shared rage and hatred. He wanted it to feed Liam's soul, to make him powerful and brave. Liam didn't feel that way most of the time. In fact, he felt exactly the opposite—helpless and powerless. But there was one time where he no longer felt that way, and that was in the flat of a couple who'd been killed. The strength it took to take another person's life, the complete power they had over another human being—there was nothing else quite like it. He'd been filled with so much anger, it was as though he couldn't control it. He didn't understand where the anger came from, but it was real. So real he'd almost blacked out from it, only to open his eyes to all that blood.

He'd been horrified but also fascinated.

He'd asked his father if they were going to do it again, and he'd asked Liam if he *wanted* to do it again.

His need, his desire, embarrassed him, but if it was a part of the war, then he should probably embrace it.

Liam read through the messages.

<Fucking whore at the supermarket looked down her nose at me today. How should I repay her?>

<Anyone managed to fuck a Stacy yet?>

<Women need to stay in the kitchen or the bedroom. Those are the only places they can be of any use.>

<Where has the Stacy and Chad killer gone? When's he going to take out another one?>

Liam took a moment and then wrote back encouraging replies. He felt like a bit of a fraud for replying. So much of what these men wrote about was about sex, and it wasn't as though he'd ever given actual sex with a woman much thought.

It was better when his dad took over. His dad knew exactly what he was doing. He seemed to be on the same wavelength as these people and gave them what they wanted.

What they really wanted was another murder.

Liam didn't know how he felt about that. That they wanted someone dead just because they looked a certain way didn't seem right to him. Just like him and his dad, and all these people online couldn't help what they looked like, surely the attractive people couldn't help it either.

He'd mentioned it to his dad one time. His father had reassured him that it was okay to question things. He'd said he wanted to raise a young man who questioned things and didn't just accept everything blindly. But he said Liam also needed to understand that he knew far more about the world and how it worked than Liam did. He'd been around for many, many more years, and he wanted Liam to have a future where he wasn't feeling like some kind of inferior subspecies to those arseholes.

Liam wasn't sure why he should be feeling inferior. Maybe if he had more interaction with people his own age, then he'd understand a bit more about his father's point of view. But he was kept away from other people most of the time. His dad said it was to protect him, that he didn't want Liam growing up the way he did—constantly vilified and bullied by boys who thought they were better than him because they were a few inches taller or were able to grow a beard years before he even had so much as a bit of bumfluff on his chin. He said the girls were even worse, laughing behind their hands, teasing him—and not in a good way. They were all a bunch of sluts and whores. Hypocritical, too. He said they'd spread their legs for any of the popular guys in school, but the minute he tried to kiss or touch them, they were all shouting rape. It wasn't as though they were innocent in any way. What difference did it make whose dick they sucked? Wasn't one penis much like the next?

Liam was old enough to know what it meant to have sex. He knew that it was impossible to get someone pregnant unless you had sex with them, too, which meant that at some point his dad must have had sex with his mother.

Though he was anxious about Dad's reaction, he hadn't been able to stop himself from mentioning this.

His father had snorted and said, "Yeah, she put out, but it didn't last. I thought she might have been different to the others, but I was wrong about that. After she fell pregnant with you, she lost all interest. To be honest, I wasn't that keen on her like that either, all fat and waddly. I couldn't do...what I wanted, knowing there was something else growing inside her. It didn't feel right. Then you were born, and she still wasn't interested. After her body went back to normal, I didn't give her much of a choice. A man has needs, you know. She tried to leave when you were about a year old. She was going to take you with her. I told her I'd kill you if she did that."

Liam had been shocked that Dad had threatened to kill him, but he'd reassured Liam that it had only been a threat and he'd never have actually done it. The point was that his mother had believed his father was capable of it, and that was what mattered.

Liam had let this information sink in. If his mother had been willing to leave him, did that mean she hadn't loved him? Or was it that she *had* loved him, and that was the reason she'd stayed away?

His dad must have picked up on his son's hesitation as he'd said that he couldn't have had Liam brought up by that slut. He said he'd rather have died himself than have a son who'd grown up like that.

A son needed a father. All those whores out there tried to make people believe that men were obsolete now, that they weren't needed, should be taught a lesson. And the men who supported them were no better. They all needed to be put in their place.

So his mother had left, and she'd never come back.

Liam guessed that meant Dad was right about women.

Did that mean it was right to kill them? A small sacrifice to make sure the others knew their place.

Still, uneasiness twisted in Liam's stomach. What if the police caught up with them? Would they both go to jail? He didn't want to get locked up, especially if he was taken somewhere without his dad. He'd be terrified. The only person he'd ever lived with before was his dad, and he couldn't imagine being surrounded by lots of other people. The thought of it sent his heart racing and his blood rushing through his ears. He'd bet they wouldn't be people who'd understand why they'd done what they'd done. Maybe some of the prison officers would even be women?

But the worst part was that he'd be separated from his dad, and then he wouldn't know what to do with himself.

Chapter Twenty-Nine

"Feeling better?" Sadie's boss asked when she went into work the following day.

She still felt guilty about pulling a sickie, but Grant's words about how easily she'd be replaced echoed in her head, too.

"Yes, much, thanks. I just needed to rest after getting it out of my system. How did the meetings go? Did anyone else take over, or were they rescheduled?"

"Yvonne took over, and she did a great job. The clients really warmed to her."

Yvonne was in her mid-forties and had been working here for the last few years. She didn't make any effort to hide that she looked down on those younger than her—especially the women. Yvonne was one of those women who'd had her children early, and then had gone back to school when they were in their teens and retrained. She always thought she knew far more about everything than the younger members of the team.

Sadie wasn't happy about the thought of Yvonne taking over her clients, but what could she do? She was the one who'd chosen to call in sick. She hoped the clients weren't going to request to deal with Yvonne in the future—that would be a real kick in the teeth.

She forced a smile. "That's great. I'm so pleased it went well. I'll be happy to take over now I'm back."

Tony glanced over at Yvonne's desk. "Well, talk to Yvonne about that. I'm not sure how she left things with them. She might have arranged to contact them at a later date."

"But they're my clients. They've always come to me."

His lips pursed. "No, Sadie, they're not your clients, they're the company's clients. You'll do whatever is best for the company, and if they've chosen to deal with Yvonne from now on, and that's what makes them happy, then that's exactly what's going to happen. If you're not pleased about it, maybe you'll have to be more careful about what you eat."

Hot tears of frustration burned the backs of her eyes. She wasn't going to cry in front of everyone.

The worst part was all this was her fault. She should have trusted her instincts not to have called in sick, but she'd allowed Grant to persuade her. How stupid she'd been. Deep down, she'd already known that something like this was going to happen. But then she remembered what Grant had said about how easily she'd be replaced in the office and realised how right he'd been. She'd been working here for almost ten years, and all it had taken was one sick day for her to end up on the bad side of her boss and the clients.

What kind of work/life balance was that?

Her frustration turned to anger. Aware she might do or say something she'd regret later, she headed for the bathrooms. They were unisex, which always annoyed her. She didn't want to share a toilet with a bloke who liked to piss all over the seat, but it wasn't as though she had much choice. She slammed into one of the stalls and then locked the door behind her. She used a piece of toilet tissue to lower down the seat and then dropped on top of it, her head in her hands.

"Fuck," she muttered to herself.

What was done was done. She couldn't go back and change things now; she was just going to have to deal with the consequences.

She wasn't looking forward to going home and telling Grant what had happened. Though she hadn't known him long, she could already tell that he'd use this as some kind of weapon to prove his point.

Maybe she just shouldn't tell him, though she wanted someone on her side.

Chapter Thirty

The days flew by, and there was nothing Erica could do to slow them down. Every lead she'd chased went to a dead end. The pressure was mounting, and it didn't help Erica feel any better.

"Boss," Hannah said, approaching her desk, "I've found Robert Brooks' sister. I don't know if you want to speak to her..."

"I do. I definitely do."

"She's already on her way in. She's keen to talk to you, too."

"Great."

A couple of hours later, Erica greeted a silver-haired woman in her fifties in reception. Erica could see the similarities in her face between her and her brother.

"DI Swift." The woman got to her feet, offering her hand. "Charlene Brooks. It's good to meet you."

They shook hands, and Erica led Charlene into one of the interview rooms.

"Can I get you a coffee or anything before we start?" Erica offered. "You've come a long way."

Charlene set her handbag down beside the chair and sat. "No, I'm fine, really, and it's only a couple of hours by train. I make the journey every time I visit Robert, so I'm used to it. I'd prefer to just get on with things. Your colleague told me on the phone that there's been a development with Robert's case?"

Erica took the chair opposite and folded her hands on the table. "I don't want to give you any false expectations. Honestly, I'm not sure what the result of this investigation is going to be, but I believe it might end up with one, if not two, people behind bars."

"You believe that Robert didn't do it?" Hope glimmered in her eyes.

"For me, there's enough doubt, but I'm not the judge or the jury. But I definitely think there's too much connecting this most recent case to the Gabriels' murder for Robert to be the one responsible."

A tear slid down Charlene's cheek, and she wiped it away. "I can't tell you how good it feels just to hear someone say they believe us. I never once thought Robert was capable of killing those people. I saw the crime scene photos, and they were...horrific. I'm not saying Robert is a perfect person. He certainly lost his temper on occasion, just like we all do, but he could never do that. I met Beatrice a number of times when she and Robert were going out. I liked her. I hated that someone could have done that to her, but it wasn't my brother. I'd swear my life on it."

Erica offered her a sympathetic smile. "Are you still in touch with Robert's solicitor?"

"Yes, though it's been a few years. We thought we'd exhausted every angle, but now this..."

"Do you know if his lawyer ever had any reason to suspect anyone else of the crime?"

"No. If we had, we might have stood a chance of getting him off. That there was literally no one else to point the finger at went against him. Everyone wanted to put someone behind bars for such a terrible crime, and that person ended up being Robert."

"I'm sorry," Erica said.

Charlene shook her head in dismay. "Having him wasting away in prison while the actual killer is out there somewhere, living his life, just felt so fucking unfair. They didn't only take Beatrice's and Jack's lives, this person took Robert's, too, in a way."

"I can't make any promise, Charlene, but if there is any way I can help to prove Robert's innocence, I'll do whatever it takes."

"Thank you, Detective. It means so much to have someone on our side."

Chapter Thirty-One

Sadie opened the front door of her flat and stepped inside. She dumped her handbag on the small kitchen table and went straight to the kettle to make herself a cup of tea. After the day she'd had, she thought she could do with something stronger, but if she started now, she was only going to end up hungover in the morning, and that was the last thing she needed. If she went into work hungover, she'd give Tony a reason to make her feel even more shit than she already did. She didn't think he'd fire her, but he could certainly make her life harder.

Grant had gone into work this morning, but he was coming back here when he'd finished. They'd been spending every moment together when they weren't at work.

The kettle rumbled and then clicked off. Steam hit the bottoms of the wall-hung kitchen cupboards, and at the back of her mind, she acknowledged that they could do with a wipe.

She busied herself by choosing a mug out of the cupboard—her favourite one for this time of day—and then plucked a teabag out of the cannister.

She was about to drop it into the cup when it struck her that something wasn't quite right.

Sadie paused, a teabag in hand, hovering it above the mug. What was different?

It suddenly hit her. Monty wasn't winding himself around her legs, yelling for his dinner. She always fed him the moment she got home. If she didn't, he wouldn't leave her alone, but tonight he was absent.

"Monty?" she called. "Where are you, puss?"

Was he still asleep? She was fully aware he spent the entire day while she was at work buried into a blanket on her bed. Oh, what a life it was to be a cat.

"Monty! Dinner!"

She paused again, waiting for the familiar thud-thud of his little feet as he jumped from the bed, but none came. His biscuit bowl—the one she filled every morning before leaving for work—was still completely full. He always ate all his biscuits during the day, only leaving the bed for short amounts of time to get a snack before going back to sleep.

Worry seeped into her heart. Was he sick?

Her tea forgotten, she left the kitchen and walked the small hallway down to her bedroom.

Sadie stopped. "Oh."

Her bedroom door was shut. That was strange. She never shut the bedroom door because Monty needed access to the kitchen for his food and water bowls, and his litter tray.

"Damn it."

A pitiful miaow came from behind the door.

She exhaled a breath, though it was only partly in relief that her pet was all right. She didn't want to think what sort of mess she was about to open her bedroom door to, considering he'd been without access to a litter tray all day.

Sadie eased open the door, careful not to hit Monty with it, in case he was standing right behind it. A streak of orange fur zipped past her shins and headed straight for the kitchen. He was probably half starved after being separated from his biscuit bowl.

Instead of going after him, she remained in the doorway, taking in her room.

Thankfully, there was no sign of any puddles or hint of a stink where he might have used her bed as a toilet. How had the door got shut? She always left it open. Could it have blown shut? No, that didn't make sense. It wasn't as though there was a cross-breeze through the flat. Could Monty have somehow knocked it shut? She guessed it was possible, though she'd never known it to happen before.

Miaowing from the kitchen reminded her that Monty still hadn't been given his wet food for dinner.

Sadie left the bedroom and went back to the kitchen. She opened the pouch of food and put it in his bowl, giving his little head a scratch as he ate. She was still puzzling how the bedroom door had ended up being shut.

Had Grant closed it before they'd left? She hadn't seen him doing it, and she couldn't see why he would, but it was the only reasonable explanation. It wasn't as though the door had just swung partially shut. The catch had caught, which meant it had been closed with enough force for that to have happened.

Maybe it shouldn't be a big deal, but the door, combined with a few other things that had happened recently, was starting to make her uncomfortable.

Had someone been in the flat while she'd been out?

Her doorbell rang, and she breathed a sigh of relief. Grant was here. He'd have a reasonable explanation, and she could stop worrying. Plus, she'd have company, which would make her feel safer. She'd never had a problem with being alone in the flat up until now, but after the murders of that poor couple not far from where she lived, she'd been antsy.

That was probably why she was reading more into silly little things than she probably should. If the double murder hadn't occurred, she most likely wouldn't have given a second thought to the door being shut or the kettle having too much water in it. Grant probably thought she was a complete basket case, and she didn't want to give him that impression. Their relationship was still so new. She didn't want to screw it up.

Sadie went to answer the door.

Grant stood on her doorstep, a bouquet of flowers hiding his face.

Instantly, she forgot all about the cat and the door.

"Oh, are they for me?"

"No, I got them for your neighbour, Mrs Smith." He made up her neighbour's name as he hadn't learnt it yet, and partially turned away from her. "I was just heading up there now."

She grabbed the flowers out of his hand and playfully smacked him on the shoulder. "Don't you dare."

He laughed. "Depriving an old lady of some flowers. How could you?"

"She'll survive." She yanked him in for a kiss. "They're beautiful, thank you."

Within minutes, they were back in bed, in a tangle of arms and legs.

It was only later, when she was lying with her head rested on his chest, that she remembered the door.

She sat up slightly so she could look into his face. "This is going to sound like a strange thing to say, but you didn't shut my bedroom door when we left this morning, did you?"

His forehead furrowed. "I don't think so. Why?"

"You don't think so? So there might be a chance you did?"

He shrugged. "I guess there might be. I didn't really think about it. I could have pulled it shut behind me. You know I live in a shared house, so I always close my bedroom door when I leave to give myself a bit of privacy. I could have done the same here subconsciously. Why is it a big deal?"

She relaxed back down against him, relieved that there was a sensible explanation.

"Oh, it's just that Monty got shut in here all day. He doesn't have any food or a litter tray in here. There weren't any accidents, thank God, but it's better if he has access to the kitchen."

"Shit, sorry, Sadie."

She smiled and shook her head. "No worries. I should have checked before we left for work."

"I'll know to make sure I don't do it in the future."

The mention of them having a future created a warm glow inside her chest, and she snuggled into him, a ball of happiness swelling inside her.

He saw them with a future together.

Chapter Thirty-Two

"Jasmin is popping over this evening," Erica told Shawn shortly before they were due to leave the office. She kept her voice low so she wasn't overheard. "I hope that's all right."

"Of course it is. Is it a social visit or work?"

"A bit of both, I think, but mainly work. She told me that we should eat first and she'd be over later."

"I'll grab some Chinese food on my way home," Shawn said. "Neither of us have had a moment to even think about shopping or cooking."

"I know. I'm so thankful Poppy gets meals over at Natasha's, otherwise she'd probably have scurvy by now." She covered her face with her hands. "I'm a terrible mother."

Erica finished up the last of her work, picked up Poppy, and headed home. Shawn arrived not long after, the promised Chinese food in hand. They ate together around the table, scraping the tubs clean.

Around eight p.m., the doorbell rang, and Erica went to answer it. As she'd expected, Jasmin stood on the doorstep.

"I can't stay long," Jas said. She had her laptop bag with her. "I just wanted to show you where I am with the incel thing."

Erica allowed Poppy to say hi and then sent her daughter upstairs. She didn't want or need Poppy knowing what kind of hatred there was in the world.

Jasmin set up at the kitchen table. "I decided the best way to get some insider knowledge about what's going down was to become one of them."

"You became one of them? How?"

"Pretty easy, really. I created a profile and joined some of their chatrooms. I've been spending some time liking their posts and making the sorts of comments I knew would draw their interest. I've been paying particular attention to any threads that mention the murders. I hate to say it, but there's a lot of them."

"Are the incels claiming responsibility for the killings?"

"Not yet. But they're certainly supporting them. Photographs of the couple have been uploaded online. There's a lot of name-calling, referring to Tabitha as a whore and slut, and pretty much any derogatory name you can think of for a woman. They're saying Tabitha got what was coming to her."

Erica shook her head in dismay. "Jesus, just because she happened to be attractive? What the fuck is wrong with these people?"

"I know, right? And they wonder why they can't get a girlfriend?"

"What do they say about the men?" Shawn asked.

"They're jealous, pure and simple. They want to be like these 'Chads', and I guess if they can't be like them, then they'd rather kill them. They've got this idea that eighty percent of the women out there only want the top twenty percent of men. There's a lot of talk about how, if they exterminated the top twenty percent of men, then women would have no choice but to date the incels."

"I'd rather stay single," Erica commented.

"Same," Jasmin said. "They hate that women have too much power in the dating sphere, that they're no longer forced to marry men they'd never even consider."

Shawn rolled his eyes. "Forced marriages. These people just get better and better."

Jasmin carried on. "Some of the men I've spoken to online want to be 'Chads' and think that if they go to the gym and get plastic surgery then they'll become one of them, while others don't believe that anything they do to improve themselves will result in gaining a romantic relationship with a woman. They think they're forever doomed to be single virgins."

"You've hidden your real identity on there?" Erica checked. "There's no way any of these people can find out who you really are and track you down? I can't imagine they'd be very happy if they discovered one of the people they'd been talking to online was actually a woman."

Erica was mindful of what had happened the last time Jasmin had helped them with a case. She'd ended up being attacked near her home.

"Don't worry. They won't find out who I really am. I've been careful."

"I don't want you to ever make yourself vulnerable for this job."

"I learned from last time," Jas said. "I promise I've covered all my tracks."

"Good."

"I've been paying particular attention to anyone who mentions either Tabitha or Jordon. Some of them are boastful about it being an incel who murdered them, but no one has actually claimed responsibility for the murders yet."

Shawn tapped his fingers on the table. "Do you think one of the people in these chatrooms might be our killer? Is there a way we could try to weed him out?"

"Maybe I could post something only the killer would know?" Jas said.

Erica thought for a moment. They didn't even know if they were on the right track with this incel stuff. While it was terrifying to learn what was going on in the minds of some of their young men, just because they were writing about the murders online didn't mean one of them had actually committed them.

She thought of something. "Maybe you could write a part of what was written on the wall of the Moots' place. See if anyone recognises it. Could you include 'I'm not strong enough' in one of your posts?"

Jasmin nodded. "Yeah, I could do that easily."

"Just because someone recognises it, doesn't mean they're the killer," Shawn said. "They could just have access to the police files."

Erica arched her brow. "If I have police officers in the Met who are also a part of this movement then I'd say that weeding them out would be a good thing. We don't need people in a position of authority who also hate women."

Jasmin gave her a side eye and lifted an eyebrow. She clearly had something to say.

"What?" Erica asked.

"There are police officers who hate all kinds of people," she said. "There are officers who target young black males, simply because of the colour of their skin. There are officers who target Muslims or Jews. It doesn't matter where you look, there are always going to be people who hate, and being in the Met doesn't rule people out of that."

As much as Erica hated it, she knew Jasmin spoke the truth.

"Okay, do it," she agreed. "Let me know if anything interesting comes up."

She caught sight of a small face peering around the corner from the stairs. "Poppy," she admonished. "How long have you been standing there?"

"Not long."

Erica checked the time. "Come on, it's time for you to go to bed."

"Can Jasmin take me?" Poppy asked hopefully.

Erica exchanged a glance with Jasmin, who grinned.

"I'd be happy to," Jas said and turned to Poppy. "Come on, mischief. Up to bed. You can read me a story."

Chapter Thirty-Three

A painfully bright light pressing against Sadie's closed eyelids demanded for her to wake.

She had no idea what the time was, but she didn't think it was morning yet. Besides, this didn't feel like sunlight, and she always closed the curtains before she went to bed. It was one of the things she found unbelievable when she watched films or television shows—that no one ever seemed to draw their curtains or blinds at night. It wasn't only that she didn't want to be woken by bright sunshine in the early hours—she also hated the idea of someone peering in at her while she slept.

She tried to squint, but the light was so blinding, everything else faded to darkness. Automatically, she twisted her face away, trying to escape it, but the light followed her like an annoying mosquito.

As her awareness of her surroundings sharpened in direct correlation to her wakefulness, something else struck her. Someone stood beside her, looming over the bed. She sensed them as much as she was able to see them—blinded as she was by the light. But they were definitely there, and some deep instinct told her the person was male.

She opened her mouth to scream, but a hand clamped over it, stifling her voice.

Was it Grant? Why would he be holding his hand over her mouth? Was he trying to keep her quiet for some reason? Her heart pounded, and she tried to push him away, but he held firm.

All her fears and worries from the past week collided with a crash of adrenaline and an internal groan of understanding.

She'd been so stupid. Why had she let a perfect stranger into her home and life? Everyone warned her to take her time, but she hadn't listened, and now this was going to be her punishment.

"Don't make a sound," the person attached to the hand growled.

A second shock wave of realisation hit her.

The person wasn't Grant.

She suddenly remembered the couple who'd been murdered, and a fresh jolt of adrenaline went through her, clearing her mind. She lashed out at the man above her, hitting and kicking. Her feet and legs were all tangled up in the duvet and made no impact. The fight meant the man had to move the light away. He'd been shining a torch in her eyes. There was enough light in the room to make out the person above her. His face and hands were covered with white gloves and some kind of protective white hood tied beneath his chin. He looked as though he was in crime scene.

Maybe he was.

The man was immovable no matter how much she tried to fight. Then his hand changed position so he was no longer only covering her mouth but her nose as well.

She tried to suck in a breath, but all she got was skin and the faint aroma of chemicals. Her lungs burned from the lack of oxygen, and her panic and struggles changed direction, moving inwards.

"Promise me you won't scream and that you'll stop fighting, and I'll let go of your nose."

Frantic, she nodded. She'd have agreed to anything at that point if it meant she could draw in air.

True to his word, he adjusted his grip and allowed her to suck in blissful oxygen. She wheezed and gasped but didn't scream.

Where was Grant?

During her struggles, she'd struck out with her left arm and leg onto what had become his side of the bed, and he hadn't been there. Was he a part of this? Did he know the man standing over her now? Had he let the stranger into her home?

Or was Grant hurt, too?

She pushed herself to sitting, and this time the man let her sit up. Her bedroom door was open, and the light was on in the entrance hall, just as it had been when she'd gone to bed.

Her flat wasn't big—far from it. It was possible to see the living room through the bedroom doorway, the small hallway an open space between the two rooms.

In the doorway of the living room, Grant was on his hands and knees. Balanced on his back was one of the used wine glasses from last night.

What the hell was he doing?

How had this man done that to him, and she hadn't even woken up? She'd had one too many glasses of red wine last night. Even now, her head felt foggy and heavy. She wasn't really sure what was happening.

The intruder stepped to the end of the bed. He addressed Grant. "If I hear that glass fall, I'll know you moved and then I'll kill her, got it?" He turned to her. "If either of you screams or tries to escape, I will kill the other one right in front of you, do you understand? Do you want that? To watch your perfect partner die in the most painful way because of something *you* did?"

He was using the love one person had for another as a way of silencing them. Of making them do his bidding.

He was going to kill them anyway.

Did she love Grant? They'd only been in each other's lives just over a week, though the week had been an intense whirlwind. Up until now, she'd have said they'd both fallen in love at first sight, that what they had was real, but now she was questioning everything. How could she love him when she barely knew him?

Was she really going to sacrifice her own life for his?

The upstairs neighbour, Mrs Whitworth, often couldn't sleep. She always complained about her insomnia, how, when she woke in the early hours of the morning, she would stay in bed and read. Could she be awake now? And if she was awake, would she hear Sadie's scream from downstairs and call the police?

A muffled whimper came from Grant. He wasn't going to do anything to save them. And if she couldn't rely on somebody else to save her then she was going to have to try to save herself, no matter the risk. She was going to die anyway. This bastard was going to kill, but first he would most likely rape her.

"No, please," she cried.

"What did I warn you of? Each time you make a noise, your boyfriend, Chad, over here gets cut."

He strode across to the other room, brisk and purposeful, and raised the knife above his head. Grant's eyes went round with fear, and the knife came down, finding purchase between his shoulder blades. The glass toppled to the floor and smashed into pieces.

Sadie managed to trap the scream of terror inside her lungs. She'd never seen someone stabbed before. It was brutal and terrifying.

The man glanced over at her, a smile of pleasure touching his lips.

"Good girl," he said, "now you're taking me seriously. Make another sound, and I'll stab Chad again."

Why does he keep calling him Chad?

Grant was bleeding on the floor. There was so much blood. She didn't want him to die, but she didn't want to die either.

The man reached the bed. She couldn't take her eyes off the bloodied knife still in his hand. With his other hand, he reached down and grabbed the elastic waistband of her knickers and yanked them down her thighs.

He glanced over his shoulder and said, "Turn away," though Grant wasn't even looking.

She didn't struggle. The threat of the blade plunging into her body was too much. Tears streamed down her face. She wished she could convince herself that he'd rape her and then leave, but she'd read the reports of what had happened to that other couple. Neither of them had made it out alive. While being compliant might save some people in this kind of situation, deep down she knew that wasn't going to save them.

Sadie sobbed, as quietly as she could.

"You see what you did?" he said. "See what you did to your perfect man?" He glanced over his shoulder again. "This is what we do to teach them how to know their place."

Who's he talking to?

She turned her face away and let him do his thing, tried not to feel his hardness stabbing inside her.

He spoke as he raped her, calling her names. "You're a fucking whore, Stacy. A dirty slut. This is all you'll ever be good for."

Stacy? Who is Stacy?

Did he have them confused with someone else?

At least he was wearing a condom, that was something to be grateful for. Not that she was going to live through this long enough for it to make any difference. Then she realised he wore it not for any fears of sexually transmitted diseases or even pregnancy. No, the reason he had gone to the effort of wearing a condom was that he didn't want to risk leaving his DNA around in the form of semen.

When he was finished with them, he'd find a new couple to kill.

Finally, he climbed off her.

"Don't move, bitch, I'm not done with you yet."

She let out a sob, and his head snapped around.

"What did I say? No noise."

He left the room once more.

This time he didn't stab Grant but slashed the sharp edge of the blade across Grant's face.

"Help, please," he whimpered, bleeding onto the floor. "Someone help us." But he was so weak, unless someone was in the room, they'd never have heard.

"You want me to cut her, too?"

"No, please," she whispered.

He stalked back over to her, the knife held high...

And brought it down in a sweeping arc, the silver blade vanishing into the soft flesh of her belly.

The pain was like nothing else she'd ever experienced. Blinding white. All encompassing. She clamped her teeth together, biting her tongue, fighting everything she had to stop the agony bursting from between her lips in a scream. How could she possibly stay quiet? But if she didn't, he was going to stab her again, and she'd do anything not to go through such utter torture again.

But then she realised her noise wouldn't get *her* stabbed again—it was going to be Grant. If she screamed, she wasn't the one who'd be punished.

How could she do it? Would people judge her? But what did that even matter if she was dead?

No one would ever have to know that she'd risked Grant's life in order to save her own.

Sadie opened her mouth, drew as much air into her lungs as possible through the pain, and screamed.

Chapter Thirty-Four

Police Constable Lisa Wirral sat in the response car with her partner, PC Gary Tomforde.

It was just gone two-thirty in the morning. It had been a quiet night so far—though no one would ever use the Q word for fear of asking for trouble—and they were sharing a packet of biscuits and a thermos of tea that Lisa had brought from home. She couldn't stand the tea from any of the service stations, or anywhere else for that matter. And if she was going to stay up all night, she needed a decent cup of tea.

A call came over the radio from dispatch.

"Nearest unit, reports of screaming, possible assault ongoing." Dispatch gave the address.

"That's us," she said, brushing biscuits crumbs off the front of her uniform.

Gary responded to dispatch to say they were going on the shout, tossed the packet into the footwell, and lit up the vehicle.

They drove to the address to find the ground-floor flat in darkness, and a worried neighbour standing on the pavement outside.

Lisa and Gary got out of the car.

"Were you the person who put in the nine-nine-nine call?" Gary asked.

"Yes," the woman said. "I was asleep, but something must have woken me. Then I heard a scream. It was woman's scream. I think it must have been my downstairs neighbour, Sadie Douglas."

"Does she live alone?" Lisa asked.

"Yes, but she's had a man hanging around lately. I've seen him coming and going all week."

"Do you know who the man is? Could he be a relative?"

"Not from the way the two of them were kissing on the street the other day."

Lisa exchanged a glance with Gary. Was this a domestic violence situation?

"Let's get inside," Gary said.

They went to the front door of the flat and knocked and rang the bell.

"Miss Douglas," Gary shouted. "It's the police. Is everything all right in there?"

"Is there rear access to the property?" Lisa asked the neighbour.

"Yes, around the side."

"I'll check it out," Gary said.

Lisa banged on the front door again. "Miss Douglas? Sadie? Can you come to the door?"

She went to the window, cupped her hand to the side of her face, and used her torch to see inside. The window gave a view into the living room. There was a dark shape on the floor, near the doorway, that was suspiciously human sized.

"Shit." She got on the radio, requesting backup and for an ambulance to be sent to the scene. Whoever was on the floor looked like they were hurt, if not worse.

A shout from the rear of the house came from her partner. "I'm in. Police!"

"Wait here," Lisa told the neighbour. "My colleagues will be here shortly."

She broke into a jog to round the side of the property. The back door stood open. Gary must have already gone inside. She hoped he'd be safe.

There was a possibility the person might still be alive. She hurried through the flat to where she'd seen the shape lying on the floor and sucked in a breath of shock. There was blood everywhere. She was still new to the job and hadn't seen as much as her partner. She staggered back, while he dropped to his knees beside the victim to start CPR.

The neighbour had reported a woman's scream, but this was clearly a man. Had the resident of the flat been the one to stab the man?

"I'll check the rest of the flat. The perpetrator might still be in here."

Directly opposite was a door to a bedroom.

"We've got a second victim!" she shouted to her partner.

Christ, where was the ambulance? From the amount of blood on the victim, plus spattered across the bed and walls, she thought they were too late anyway.

Something else caught her eye. Writing on the wall.

You need to stop him.

It was written in blood.

The figure on the bed let out a groan.

"I've got one alive!" she shouted, adrenaline hitting her system like a syringe of heroin. "I think it's probably Sadie Douglas."

Her partner was busy trying to do whatever he could for the male victim before the ambulance arrived, performing CPR and trying to stop the bleeding.

She climbed on the bed, only caring about keeping Sadie alive until the paramedics arrived.

"Sadie, my name is Lisa. I'm a police officer. I'm going to take care of you, okay? You're going to be all right."

She wanted to ask the injured woman who had done this to her, if she could tell her anything about what had happened, but the sheer volume of blood prevented any questions from emerging from her lips.

Lisa remembered the murders that had happened only a week earlier. The couple that had been found stabbed to death in their homes. Something had been written on the wall then, hadn't it, though that information hadn't been released to the public. This had to be the same killer.

There was a large stab wound to the victim's abdomen. She balled some of the sheets and used them to apply pressure to the cut, trying to staunch the flow of blood.

"Stay with me, Sadie. You're safe now. An ambulance is on the way. You're going to be just fine."

She had no idea if she was or not, but it felt like the right thing to say. Would this poor woman still be alive when the ambulance got here? Lisa had no idea.

"Do you know the person who did this to you?"

A word creaked from between the victim's bloodied lips. "Graa..."

"Graa?" Lisa echoed. "Who's that? The person who stabbed you?"

Sadie's eyelids flickered.

Lisa raised her voice. "Look at me, Sadie. You're doing great. Keep looking at me."

The man on the floor in the other room must have been her boyfriend. If she survived this, she was then going to have to go through the pain and grief of finding out he hadn't lived.

She tried to stay focused on speaking to the victim and keeping the pressure down on the wound. Sadie was still losing blood. She couldn't handle this. She wasn't good enough. This poor woman was going to die, and it would be Lisa's fault. If only she'd been the one who'd gone to the man and she'd let her partner find Sadie instead, then maybe Sadie would live.

This was all too much. She was only twenty-three. She should be out partying with her friends, not trying to hold blood inside a victim.

Lisa wanted to cry, but instead bit down on the sides of her tongue until it hurt. There would be plenty of time for losing her shit later, when all of this was over, and she was left alone with her thoughts, but right now, she needed to remember her training and stay calm.

Chapter Thirty-Five

The mobile phone on the bedside table on Erica's side of the bed rang into the dark room, the screen lighting up.

Automatically, she checked the time. It was just after three a.m., which meant something serious had happened for her to be contacted.

"Swift," she answered, keeping her voice low, though Shawn was already awake beside her.

He turned on the bedside lamp on his side. He frowned at her as she listened to what the voice on the other end of the line told her.

"I'll be right there," she said and ended the call.

"There's been another one," she told him, already swinging her legs out from under the covers and planting her bare feet on the floor. "A young couple stabbed in their home."

"Fuck. Does it look like it's the same perpetrator?"

She nodded. "Something's been written on the wall in blood."

"Goddammit." He climbed out of bed as well and grabbed his clothes. "What's the address? I'll take Poppy to your sister's and then meet you there."

"You sure?" she checked.

"Absolutely. You need to get there first."

"Thanks, Shawn."

He took her hand and kissed her lightly on the cheek. "Of course. That's what partners do, right?"

She was so grateful to have him in her life.

Erica took a few minutes to use the bathroom, brush her teeth, and drag her hair back into a ponytail, and then she was out the door and in the car. Her mind raced, her heartbeat knocking against her ribs. Had the same killer struck again, or was this a copycat? She thought of the online incel chatter, supporting the murderer and encouraging others to do the same. It was more than possible that someone had decided to take them up on that.

The only thing that didn't fit was the words left on the wall. That was a piece of information they'd kept from the press, so either there had been a leak, or the actual killer had fed this piece of information online somewhere for his admirers to copy, or this was the same culprit. Or had Jas managed to add it to one of the online chats, like they'd agreed?

It had barely been a week since the first killing. Had his taste for death grown legs? She remembered the words written on the wall of Tabitha and Jordon Moots' home.

You have to stop him.
I'm not strong enough.

Did that mean whoever wrote them knew he was going to kill again? That the frequency of the murders would pick up pace?

She arrived at the road where the latest victims had been attacked.

Flashing lights swept across the still-dark sky. Lights were on inside many of the homes, the neighbours curious about what was happening on their street to warrant so many police.

Erica felt sick about there being a second attack. Though she'd worried there might be, deep down she'd hoped she'd just been paranoid.

She looked around for the sergeant in charge of the scene and spotted Sergeant Carys Jones.

"Sorry to get you out of bed at this time," Jones said.

"Have there been any recent developments? Is the female victim still alive?"

"For the moment, yes. One of our officers, PC Lisa Wirral, did an excellent job of keeping her stable until the ambulance arrived. She's been taken to the Royal London Hospital."

"Will she make it?"

"Honestly, I don't know. She's lost a lot of blood and had multiple stab wounds."

"And the male. What's his name?"

"He didn't make it. He was already dead when our responding officers arrived. Currently, he's unidentified."

Erica frowned. "None of the neighbours know who he is?"

"No, though they said they've seen him with the female victim over this past week. We're still searching the property. Hopefully, we'll find a wallet or something else that'll tell us who he is."

"Or we hope the female victim wakes up and is able to tell us."

Jones grimaced. "Let's not pin our hopes on that."

Erica hoped Sadie Douglas survived, not only because it would be a tragedy for the killer to have claimed another life, but also because it would mean they'd have an eyewitness. She might be able to give them a description of the man who had attacked her. She might even know who he was. That kind of information would be invaluable to the case, and not only that, it would give them a solid chance of putting him behind bars before he hurt anyone else. This person had clearly got a taste for taking a life, and who knew how soon he might strike again if they didn't catch him first.

Erica glanced up at the property. "Any chance they've got security cameras?"

"Not that we've found so far."

The recent popularity of camera doorbells meant they were sometimes able to catch a clip of a suspect passing by a house, even if it wasn't the victim's. The images could be of surprisingly good quality, certainly good enough to recognise someone and for that footage to be used in court. There were a lot of houses on this street, so there was still a possibility they'd find someone with footage.

"What about witnesses?"

Jones nodded over to where one of the uniformed police officers was chatting to a lady who appeared to be in her seventies. "That's the neighbour who called nine-nine-nine. She heard a scream come from downstairs and then a crash and a door slamming. She said the scream was blood-curdling—her exact words—and knew that someone must have been very badly hurt. That was why she called us."

"She was right to," Erica said.

Another car, the headlights illuminating the now busy street, turned into the road. It stopped at the roadblock the uniformed police had created, and then one of the officers waved the vehicle through.

The car stopped on the side of the street, and the headlights darkened. Erica recognised it as belonging to Shawn. She was glad he was here now, too. She hoped everything had gone to plan with dropping off Poppy.

He signed in with the officer on the outer cordon and then joined them. All it took was a moment of eye contact and a brief nod to tell her that Poppy was fine. It felt good that he knew her well enough to understand that she needed that tiny moment of reassurance to be able to focus on the case.

She filled him in on everything she'd learned so far. They slipped easily back into work mode—where she was his DI and he was her sergeant.

"One of the victims is still alive?" he checked.

She nodded. "Last we heard. She's not doing so well, though. We think Sadie Douglas screamed, and that was why the killer ran. He must have been worried that she'd been heard, which she had. It was the upstairs neighbour who called it in. The attending officers found the back door unlocked, so the killer must have let themselves out that way. It's most likely that they got in that way, too."

Shawn pressed his lips into a line. "So Sadie screamed, but Tabitha didn't?"

"That we know of. Tabitha might have screamed, but no one heard her."

"Would the killer have risked hanging around to find out?"

Erica grimaced. "Possibly not." She turned to the sergeant. "What about how the killer got into the home?"

"Just like with the Moots' property, there's no sign of a break-in, though the back door was open. The key was in the lock on the inside of the door, so there's a possibility they just let themselves out that way to make an escape. There's no obvious sign of forced entry. No broken windows or locks."

"If he ran, he must have been covered in blood," Shawn said. "Someone must have seen something."

It might be the early hours of the morning, but that didn't mean no one was around. London was the city that never slept and, though the largest portion of the population was tucked up in their beds, there were plenty of night workers, taxi drivers, and students out partying who were still very much awake.

They needed to check each and every camera around the area, from traffic and street cams, to private CCTV. With such a precise time, it would make things easier to narrow down. They could put out a public appeal to find out if anyone had seen anything.

Fear would spread across this part of London. One double murder had been bad enough, but at least then people had been able to convince themselves that the killer had been known to the victims. Now there had been a second attack, and it meant that anyone could fall prey to this psychopath. People would be locking their doors a little more carefully at night, but, so far, a locked door hadn't been enough to keep out the murderer.

"Let's take a look at the scene," Erica said, pulling up the hood of her protective outerwear.

Sergeant Jones led them into the flat. "We'll go to the male victim first. He's through here."

The man's dark hair was matted with blood. He lay facedown on the carpet in only a pair of bloodied boxer shorts. The whole of his bare back was red with blood. There was a stab wound between his shoulder blades.

A wine glass was broken beside him. Erica wasn't sure if the red liquid on the glass was wine or blood.

"As I mentioned before, he's currently unidentified," Jones said. "He appears to be in his thirties, approximately six feet tall and around ninety kilos."

"Has he been moved?" Erica asked.

"The main area of blood is around the body. There are a few spatter marks across the rug and some of the furniture, but there's nothing else to indicate that he was moved, or even that he tried to run or crawl away. The stab wound must have fatally injured him. The other wounds are more superficial."

Erica pressed her lips together and shook her head. "I think he promised them something. Maybe told them he wouldn't hurt them if they did what he said. The promise of survival is an excellent motivator. When some people are in a life-threatening situation, all they have is hope, and maybe this killer gives it to them. They believe that if they do what he says, then he'll let them live."

Shawn gestured at the body. "But at some point, he starts stabbing. Why does the other one not run for help then?"

"It's impossible to know how people will react in situations. Maybe they were frozen in fear and horror? Maybe they clung to the possibility that the same thing wouldn't happen to them? Maybe they did run, but he caught them, and put them back in position before he killed them?"

"If Sadie ever wakes up, she might be able to tell us," Shawn said.

"Yes, if she wakes up *and* has a memory of what happened. Some people block out traumatic experiences to protect themselves. We can't rely on her telling us what happened." Erica turned her attention back to the unidentified man. "We need to find out his identity. We're looking at him as a victim right now, but how do we know he didn't play a role in this?"

"We're working on it," Jones said. "We've fingerprinted him but he's not in our system. There's no sign of a wallet yet. There's the chance the killer took it with them."

"Let's check the cars parked outside. One of them might be registered to our male victim, so we can at least get a name. He could have loved ones out there who will be missing him."

Jones nodded. "Good idea."

"Let's go into the bedroom," Erica said.

It was only a matter of a few steps from the living room to the bedroom. The flat was compact, but that was normal around these parts. Landlords and property developers wanted to get the most for their money and often divided what would have once been large family homes into much smaller flats.

She stared down at the blood-soaked mattress. The scene was almost identical to the Moots' case.

"I think it's highly unlikely this is a copycat killing," she said. "We can't rule it out completely, but I'd say it's the same perpetrator, or perpetrators, responsible for both crimes. We didn't give out the amount of detail for someone to recreate it so perfectly. Information such as the message and the exact positions of the bodies was never released. Unless this is someone who has inside information, but I hope that's not the case."

Erica stood in position at the end of the bed, facing the open doorway.

"You can see the man's body from the bed," she commented. "Was that deliberate?"

Shawn turned to her. "What do you mean?"

"Was he using the fact they could see each other, see what he was doing to the other person, as a way of controlling them? Part of the reason we thought there might be two people involved in the Moots' killing was because neither of them tried to run away or scream for help. Was that because they were frightened about what he might do to the other person?"

"It's possible, except it didn't work in this case. Sadie screamed."

"Yes, she did. Perhaps she couldn't help herself."

Erica caught sight of a photograph in a frame on the bedside table. It was of a beautiful young blonde woman and an older man—her father, Erica assumed. She thought of the first victim, Tabitha. She'd been beautiful, too.

Was that what attracted the killer to them?

Chapter Thirty-Six

Erica called her team into the office.

"Apologies for bringing you all in so early, but as I'm sure you've heard by now, there's been a second attack on a couple." She brought them all up to speed on what they knew so far about the murder and attempted murder. "The last word I received was that Sadie Douglas is in surgery and is critical. Let's hope she'll recover and will be able to give us a statement, but we can't rely on that."

Jon put up his hand. "Do we think it's the same perpetrator then?"

"Or perpetrators," she said. "It certainly seems that way, though this time they must have made a more rapid exit as the neighbour called the police after Sadie Douglas screamed. They still took the time to write on the wall in what we think is her blood, however."

Erica pointed to a photograph of the writing, which was positioned next to the one from the Moots' home. "As you can see, the handwriting is identical. We have local police searching the area for anyone suspicious. There is still no sign of a murder weapon. The postmortem should be able to tell us if the same style of knife was used in the stabbings, though of course, it won't be able to tell us if it was the exact same knife."

"Have we found the murder weapon yet?" Hannah asked.

"No, so far it would appear the killer has taken the knife with them. We need to ask ourselves why is that? Is it because they plan on using it again?"

The implication that there might be a third attack weighed heavy in the room.

Erica gave it a moment and then said, "We will be launching an appeal to the public for anyone who might have seen someone suspicious in the Bow area during the early hours. Anyone who might have dashcam footage or security footage that might have caught him on the run. There's a good chance his clothes were bloodied, and if they were, it means he's more likely to get noticed."

"What if he had a vehicle parked nearby?" Hannah suggested.

"That's a strong possibility. We need to go over all the traffic cam footage from the time as well. The good thing is that we have an almost exact time, which will help us narrow things down. It's going to be a tedious job, but I want every single vehicle caught on camera accounted for. Find out who was driving, where they were going, what they were doing out at that time. Do any of the drivers have criminal records that we need to be aware of? If this person fled the property and jumped straight into a car or van, then there will be evidence of blood on the seats and on the door handle. If a vehicle has been recently cleaned, then that should raise a red flag. We need to catch this bastard before he strikes again."

"Do you think he will kill again?" Jon asked.

"I think he'll try, yes. As soon as he learns that Sadie Douglas survived, he'll realise whatever sick need he has wasn't sated. I imagine he's anxious and unfulfilled. He'll want to try again, perhaps to prove to himself that he can."

"Maybe he won't," Jon threw back. "This might have scared him. Perhaps he'll withdraw and go into hiding."

"That's also a possibility, and let's hope that's true, at least for the sake of whoever his next victims might be."

"It looks as though he has a type." Erica gestured to the photographs of the victims. "Both sets of victims were in their early thirties, white, attractive, professional individuals. Going back to the Robert Brooks case, the female victim had similar appearance. I can't help but wonder if there's anything to this incel chatter online. I've got Jasmin Webb working on it, but we don't have anything solid yet."

Erica checked the time. It was approaching six a.m., so almost a reasonable hour to call someone. She'd get Jasmin in here in case something came up that gave them a solid lead to follow.

Right now, they needed all the help they could get.

Chapter Thirty-Seven

A steady beep filtered through to her subconscious. Sadie recognised the sound but couldn't place it. Was it her alarm? Had she set it to go off for work? She had no idea what day it was and certainly didn't know what time it was. Was she late?

Her throat hurt. She couldn't swallow. She couldn't open her eyes either. Her throat wasn't the only thing that hurt. Pain radiated up through her torso. No, no, no. That wasn't good. What had happened? Why was she in so much pain?

She couldn't remember anything that had happened. Was she lying in her own bed, at home? She didn't think so, but she also couldn't place her location.

Grant!

His name burst into her head like a bird exploding from a bush. Where was he? Something terrible had happened to him, she was sure. She couldn't remember what, but the knowledge embedded in her chest.

Had she done something to him? Why was she even considering that? She'd never hurt someone, would she? Not someone she cared about.

A male voice spoke somewhere nearby.

"I think she's waking up. She's crying."

Was that her father's voice? She hadn't spoken to him in so long, she struggled to remember what it sounded like. Hearing his voice was proof that she must be dreaming. Why would her father be here?

His voice came again. "Her hands are shaking, too. What does that mean?"

A stranger's voice sounded this time—a female one. "It could just be a reaction to all the anaesthesia, but she might also be gaining some awareness."

"Is she in pain?" he asked.

"Possibly some. I'll see if the doctor will increase her morphine."

There was concern in the stranger woman's voice. It made Sadie want to weep. Something truly terrible had happened.

Why couldn't she remember?

Chapter Thirty-Eight

Erica looked down at the woman in the bed.

Sadie had just come out of surgery, and forensics had already taken samples from beneath her nails and skin. A rape kit would need to be conducted, but not until Sadie had regained consciousness and could give her consent.

The worst of her wounds were hidden beneath the white sheet of the hospital bed, but Erica had seen the photographs. Sadie Douglas was lucky to be alive. She might not think that when she found out that her boyfriend was dead.

She was doing her best to be patient, but Sadie was the only witness to a murder and her own horrific attack, and there was a possibility she had seen the person who'd come into her home. If she'd got a good look at him, she might be able to give the police a description. Hell, she might even be able to give them a name if the person was already known to her.

It wasn't only the stabbing of Sadie and Grant that they wanted this person for—it was also the murders of Tabitha and Jordon Moots. There was no doubt in Erica's mind that it was the same perpetrator for both cases. Forensics were still working on Sadie's flat, but the words written in blood had been enough to tie them together.

If the killer ran, then when did he write on the wall? Before he'd stabbed the victims? In between? Why write about wanting to stop and then carrying on anyway? Was he like an alcoholic who just couldn't say no to that next drink? Was he battling something inside himself?

Or was there a second person, someone who'd taken the time to scrawl the words, perhaps even after the killer had left?

It was a puzzle, but one Erica was determined to piece together.

Sadie's father had been here when Erica had first arrived, but the man had been of little use. He'd said he hadn't spoken to Sadie in months and that they weren't close. There had been a lot of loss in her life, with her sister killing herself when they were just kids, and then her mother dying when Sadie was in her twenties.

Her father knew nothing about any men in his daughter's life, or anything about any problems she might have had recently. Erica had sent him away to get a coffee and take a break, and the man had seemed relieved to have an excuse to go.

A young man in a white coat entered the room.

"How is she, Doctor?" Erica asked him. "Any signs of her waking up yet?"

"Yes, there have been signs, but honestly, I'd rather we kept her asleep, at least for the next couple of days, until she's had some time to heal. I can't say what kind of damage it would do to her to have to relive what she's gone through so soon."

"But he's still out there. Whoever did this has killed three other people, and there's a possibility he'll do it again. If Sadie—Miss Douglas—is able to give us a description or even a name, it could make the difference between us catching him or him doing it again."

"You're a detective. I'm afraid you'll have to find some other way of catching him."

"Do you have a partner, Doctor?" Erica asked.

"Yes, I'm married. Three years in August."

"Would you be saying the same if you knew it was going to be you and your wife who the killer came for next? Or would you be waking Sadie up at the very first opportunity?"

He glanced at the floor and shook his head. "My priority always needs to be with my patient, Detective. I'm sorry."

Erica ground her molars in frustration. Maybe he was right, and she did need to move her investigative work away from Sadie, but all it might take was a matter of seconds, just enough for Sadie to whisper a name or a description. While it would have been dark in the flat during the attack, the killer would have been in there long enough for Sadie to have got some impression of him. Just finding out if there was one assailant or two would be something.

There was the possibility Sadie wouldn't remember anything at all. Sometimes the brain shuts out traumatic experiences as a way of protecting itself, and experiences don't get much more traumatic than what Sadie had been through. Erica couldn't imagine the sort of pain she would be in, too.

The doctor was right, but more than a week had passed since the attack on the Moots, and now there had been a second one. What if a third was only around the corner? She hated to think this person—or persons—were out there, walking around like a regular member of the public.

The more time that went by without her catching them, the more opportunity that gave them to do it again.

Erica's phone rang, and she stepped out of the room. It was Hannah Rudd.

"I think we've got an ID on the second victim," Hannah said down the line. "A couple of Sadie's colleagues came forward to tell us that Sadie told them she had a new man called Grant. They said they'd warned her off jumping in with someone so fast, but then she hadn't really talked about him again. We've matched that name with a silver Volkswagen Passat that's registered in the name Grant Cipri."

"What do we know about him?" Erica asked. "Is there any reason to suspect Grant of being involved in this?"

"Unsure. He has a lot of debt and currently has no fixed address, but there's no criminal record."

"He was homeless?"

"Looks like he was living out of his car. To be fair, it is a nice car."

"Debt is a good motive to commit a crime. Maybe he was paid to let someone into the flat?" Erica suggested.

"If that is the case, it didn't end well for him. I've requested everything I can about him—phone records and bank statements—and the car has been towed by forensics, too. We don't know yet if he has any next of kin."

Had the relationship between Grant and Sadie been real, or had Grant just been after a place to stay and decided that Sadie, as a successful, attractive woman with her own home, was a good option?

Chapter Thirty-Nine

Erica went back into the office. Jasmin was already there, set up with her laptop.

"I'm sorry to hear there's been another murder," Jas said.

"Yeah, me, too. Has there been anything new online that might indicate someone is involved?"

"Nothing specific to the second attack," she said. "Yet, anyway. They're encouraging the perpetrator to kill again, though. They go as far as to refer to the murderer as a hero and say that anyone who does the same is being heroic, too."

"Men who rape and murder are heroic?" Erica couldn't help the disbelief in her voice.

"Some of them are saying that for a woman to deny a man sex is like reverse rape. That it's just as harmful as a man raping a woman."

Erica's jaw dropped. "You've got to be kidding?"

"Nope. They actually convince themselves this kind of bullshit is true."

"Unbelievable."

Jasmin tapped the laptop screen. "There's one profile I keep coming back to. I'm not sure what it is about him that's catching my attention, but he just seems...different. Like one minute he's posting really angry, hate-filled comments, and then an hour later the tone is different. He starts asking questions, and look, the spelling isn't quite right with certain words."

Erica cocked her head. "Poor grammar isn't exactly unusual on the internet."

"True, but why an hour before have perfect English? Read this..."

Erica leaned in to see the screen.

<Fucking Chads and Stacys have got it coming. They deserve everything they get. Who's with me? We're at war with those fucking whores. They all deserve to be raped.>

"Jesus," Erica said, shaking her head.

"Now read this one," Jas said.

<If we hurt them, won't they hurt us? Why would anyone love us if we hate them?>

Erica frowned. "And those are from the same account?"

"Yeah. And they go on and on, one minute spouting hatred, and then these little comments filter through."

"Can you see when the profile was set up?"

"Sure. In twenty thirteen."

"Can you get talking to him? See if he's local."

"I can try. I don't know if he'll engage, though. He seems pretty inconsistent."

"Thanks, Jas." Erica patted the younger woman on the shoulder. "I appreciate you spending your time on this."

"Of course."

Erica remembered the meeting she'd had with the handwriting specialist, how he'd given her a whole heap of contradicting information. The writing had been childlike yet hadn't been written by a child. Was impulsive but also organised. Was aggressive and from a sharp mind.

Hadn't Professor Reed said the writing style had reminded him of something? He'd promised to get back to her about it, but she'd never heard from him, and she hadn't thought to follow it up.

She placed the call, but it went through to an answerphone.

"Professor Reed," she said, "It's DI Swift. I wondered if you have any more information for me about that handwriting I got you to look at. We've had another murder, so if there was anything else, I'd appreciate hearing from you sooner rather than later."

She left her number again, just in case he'd lost it, and ended the call.

Chapter Forty

The beeping grew louder.

Sadie needed to know what was happening to her. Staying trapped in this darkness wasn't an option. It was time to wake up now. She needed to face the truth.

It was bright—the light reminding her of something terrible—but she somehow managed to open her eyes.

"Dad?" she said weakly.

Beside the bed, her father leapt to his feet. "Sadie, honey, I'm so glad you're awake."

That her dad was here was almost as unsettling as not having any memory of what had happened to her.

"Where am I?" Her throat hurt, and her voice was raspy. "What am I doing here."

"You're in hospital, sweetheart. There was an...incident."

"Incident? What kind of incident?" She tried to move, to sit up, and white-hot agony flashed up through her torso, stealing her breath. "Jesus Christ."

Her father grabbed something hanging from the drip stand. "Here. You can press this button if you get too much pain. It gives you a little extra morphine."

She didn't hesitate in pushing it. Had she been sick? Had she had some kind of operation? Been in a car crash?

She couldn't remember...

Grant!

What had happened to Grant? Why wasn't he here? If something bad had happened to her, she was sure he'd be waiting at her bedside, wanting to make sure she got better again.

"Where's Grant?" she said, though she knew her dad would have no idea who Grant was. She hadn't even considered introducing the two men, and that wasn't because it had still been early in the relationship. Her father had been estranged from her for long enough that she hadn't even given it any thought.

Yet her dad's gaze shifted away, his lips thinned, as though the mention of Grant's name had made him uncomfortable. How could it, though, if he didn't even know who Grant was?

Unless Grant had tried to come and sit with her, to find out how she was, and her father had sent him away? Yes, that must have been what happened. She clutched to the explanation like a drowning person at a life raft. In the back of her head, the truth tried to drive through, and she fought against it. Her heart started to race, her breath coming quicker.

Something really terrible had happened.

"Dad?" she said, her voice sounding small, almost childlike.

He patted her hand. "Maybe I should get the doctor?"

She panicked at the thought of being left alone. "No, please don't go."

It had been many years since she'd needed him, but now the idea of being left alone in this strange hospital bed terrified her.

He looked anxiously towards the door, as though still planning an escape, but then a soft smile touched his lips, and he took her hand fully and sat back down in the chair.

"Sadie, honey, I'm afraid I've got some bad news."

Chapter Forty-One

Erica got a call from the hospital.

"You're in luck, Detective. Sadie Douglas has regained consciousness and is talking."

Erica resisted punching the air. "I'll be right there."

She drove to the hospital as fast as she dared. When she arrived at the hospital room, Sadie was already sitting up in bed. Considering the injury she'd endured, it was incredible that she'd made such a rapid recovery.

Erica knocked lightly on the door.

"Hi, Sadie, my name is Erica Swift. I'm the leading investigator on your case. I realise this is extremely difficult for you, but I do need to ask you some questions."

"Someone broke into my flat." Tears streamed down her cheeks.

"I know. I'm here to try to find out who." Erica turned her attention to Sadie's father. "Can you give us a minute?"

"Of course." He smiled at his daughter. "I'll be right back."

Erica took the chair he'd just vacated, the seat still warm beneath her.

"I let it happen," Sadie sobbed. "Oh God." She was crying so hard, she could barely breathe. "He said if I made any noise, he would stab Grant. He told Grant that if he made a sound or tried to move, I was the one who'd be stabbed. He even balanced a glass on Grant's back and told him that if it fell and broke, he'd kill me."

Understanding dawned on Erica. So that was why they'd found the broken glassware and crockery in the previous crime scenes.

Sadie kept talking, blurting it all out. "But I opened my mouth and screamed. I wanted to live. Even though I knew what it meant, that he'd kill Grant, I still did it."

"You saved yourself. There's nothing wrong with that, Sadie. You lived, and, if you'd made a different decision, you wouldn't have."

"Grant might have lived, though. He might have spared him."

Erica shook her head. "No, he wouldn't have. This person would have killed you both. He only left because you screamed and he was worried someone would hear and call the police, which they did. If you hadn't done that, you'd both be dead."

"You don't know that."

"I do, because he's done this before. You're not the first victims, Sadie. The couple who came before you died."

She gulped a sob. "Oh God, I remember now. The couple who died last week."

"That's right."

"It was the same person?"

"We believe so, yes, though we still have to prove that, and that's where you come in. I know it's hard to think back to what happened, but that's exactly what I need you to do. I'm going to need you to tell me everything you can remember. Every tiny detail, no matter how irrelevant you think it might be. We want to catch this man, Sadie, before he can hurt anyone else."

Sadie nodded and wiped her tears. "What if he comes after me again? He might want to keep me quiet?"

"You're going to have a police officer stationed right outside your door. They won't let anyone in or out unless we know who they are, okay? You are perfectly safe here."

"What if you don't catch him by the time I go home? I can't have the police follow me around for the rest of my life." She put her face in her hands. "Christ, what am I even saying? I can't go home. How can I ever step foot in that flat again after what happened? I'll never be able to sleep in that bed. I'm not sure I'll ever be able to sleep anywhere without being terrified I'll be woken up by that monster shining a torch in my eyes."

Erica frowned. "Shining a torch in your eyes?"

She nodded. "Yes, that's what he did. One minute I was sound asleep, and the next there was a bright light in my face. At first, I thought it was Grant, and I didn't know what he was doing..."

She swallowed and turned her face away.

Erica remained silent, allowing Sadie to regather her emotions and carry on.

"I-I thought it might have been him at first. I thought Grant was doing something horrible to me. That I shouldn't have trusted him in the first place."

"What made you think that?"

"Probably because I'm a total bitch. I wanted to trust him more than anything, but there was still this little part of me that couldn't bring myself to do it. Even though he was a lovely person and really seemed to care about me, I couldn't quiet this little voice in the back of my head that told me it was all an act and that things would go horribly wrong at any moment."

Was this a case of a woman naturally trying to protect her heart? Or did Grant actually have something to do with what had happened? It hadn't ended well for him, but that might have been because someone was trying to cover their tracks.

"Can you think of any specific incidents that made you suspicious of him?" Erica asked gently.

"I don't think I was suspicious of him exactly..." She let out a shaky breath. "I don't know. There were moments where I wasn't sure he was telling me the truth. Or he left out details about his life that he didn't want me to know. I think a part of it was that he was embarrassed. I earn more money than him and already own my own place, where he was still flat-sharing."

"He told you he was flat-sharing?"

Sadie's eyes widened. "Yes, he did? Wasn't he? Please don't tell me he was married."

"He wasn't. He was homeless. We believe he may have been living out of his car before he started staying with you."

"Oh God. That makes so much sense. Why didn't he ever tell me?"

"He was probably ashamed. He had a lot of debt, too. It might have been that he didn't want you to think badly of him." Erica left out that debt could also be a good reason for someone to commit a crime. "Is there anything else you can think of that made you suspicious?"

Sadie clutched her hand to the place above her heart. "I feel so awful speaking about him like this when he's..."

"I understand, but we really do need to know every detail. It could be important to finding out who did this. To making sure they don't go on and hurt anyone else."

Sadie sniffed and nodded. "I understand. There were times when I thought he'd come back to my flat when he said he was at work. He denied it, of course, but I've lived alone for so long that I know my own home. I have a certain way of doing things. I'd come home and items would have been put back in different places, like the toilet roll would be hanging the wrong way, or a cushion that's always on the sofa would be on the chair. One time, the kettle was overfilled, and my cat was shut in the bedroom. I know it's stupid, but I kept noticing these things."

"Did you ever ask Grant about it?"

"Yeah, and he just said he must have moved it before we went out or something. He just shrugged it off, but he said he hadn't come home."

"Home? Was he calling it home by then, too? The two of you hadn't been together very long."

"Our relationship got very intense very quickly. No, it wasn't his home, but he did stay there most nights from the moment we met. Don't judge, Detective. I was lonely, and we had an instant connection. Neither of us wanted to spend time outside of work without being in each other's company." Tears streamed down her face. "And I really don't think he had anything to do with what happened, if that's the route you're going down. I had a suspicious mind, but that wasn't his fault. I let him down. Right in his final moments, I let him down. He must have known that of me. His last thoughts must have been how he'd made a mistake believing I was someone he could have loved."

Erica patted the back of her hand, trying to offer some support. "I'm sure he didn't think that. If he loved you, all he would have been thinking about was you getting away. He'd have wanted you to do whatever it took."

"Yes, but that's the problem, isn't it? I didn't do the same. I didn't think that I'd do whatever it took so that he survived. I was only thinking about myself. I don't think I actually loved him. That's what the killer was working on, what he was betting on. He thought we'd love each enough, that neither of us would risk the other person's life, but I simply didn't love Grant enough."

"Don't beat yourself up."

Had the killer known that they'd only just met? Or had he seen them together and assumed they were a couple who'd been in each other's lives for years? That they'd sacrifice themselves for their loved one. From an outsider's point of view, they probably had given the impression of a couple who lived together.

"He stayed quiet for me, though," she sobbed. "He did it for me."

Erica's heart went out to her.

"What about the person who attacked you? Do you have any idea who they might be?"

"No, I'm sorry. I didn't know him."

"Him? It was definitely a man?"

"Yes, he...assaulted me."

"I'm so sorry, Sadie."

She sniffed but didn't reply.

Erica hated continuing, but she had no choice. "Was there anything distinctive about him? Anything at all you can remember?"

"I'm not sure. He was white, young, probably under thirty, though it was dark so it was hard to tell. He had his clothes and hair covered with a white plastic suit, so it was hard to get a look at him. He unzipped the front of it to..." She swallowed hard. "Rape me. I think his hair was dark, though."

"What about build? Height? Weight?" Erica prompted.

"Average for both. Maybe five feet ten. Not much more."

"Did he speak to you? Did he have an accent?"

Sadie thought for a moment. "Local, maybe. London."

"That's good, Sadie. You're doing really well. This is all very helpful. What about any distinguishing marks? Scars or tattoos? Or was he wearing any jewellery? Anything that might help us distinguish him from another person on the street."

She shook her head. "I really don't know. I'm sorry. He did his best to keep the torch shining in my face, so it was hard to see him, and he was wearing that white suit."

"A white suit like coveralls a decorator might wear?"

"No, it was more like a plastic one."

Like someone in a crime scene, Erica thought, though technically forensics suits weren't plastic but made from polyethylene.

"And was he on his own?" Erica checked.

"Yes, I think so..." Sadie hesitated. "Now you say it, he did say some strange stuff. Like he was talking to someone else."

"Do you think there might have been a second person there?"

"I didn't see anyone, but maybe." Sadie pressed the balls of her hands into her eye sockets. "Christ, I don't know what to think. It was all so crazy. I was terrified, and it was dark, and he had that fucking torch." She seemed to think of something. "I don't know if he thought we were someone else?"

Erica frowned. "Why do you say that?"

"He used names, but not our names. He kept calling me Stacy, and he was calling Grant Chad."

The names filled Erica with dread, but still, she wanted to be sure.

"Stacy is similar to Sadie," she said. "Do you think he might have just misheard someone calling you Sadie, or you misheard him?"

"I-I really don't know."

"No, of course not. I'm just thinking out loud. And of course, Grant sounds nothing like Chad."

There didn't seem to be any other explanation. Stacy and Chad were the names the incels used for men and women who fit what they viewed as being the 'perfect' genetically made-up people. The ones who won the genetic lottery at birth—the same ones they'd convinced themselves they'd missed out on. They saw 'Stacys' as being blonde, big-boobed bimbos, and 'Chads' as being the tall, squared-jawed male opposite.

Was that the reason Sadie and Grant had been targeted? From the photographs Erica had seen, it was fair to say they made an attractive couple. Was that really a strong enough reason to brutally murder and rape someone, though?

Was there ever a good enough reason?

Had Tabitha and Jordon Moots been killed for the same reason? She already knew that the deaths had stirred up chatter online with these pathetic people who saw themselves as incels, but had that been the motive behind the Moots' murder, or had they been killed by someone else, and this second attack was a copycat killing, spurred on by these incels?

"Had you received any threatening messages or calls or letters in the days or weeks leading up to the attack?" Erica asked Sadie.

She shook her head. "No, nothing like that. Honestly, this last week or so hasn't exactly been normal for me. I'd-I'd met Grant—" Her voice broke, and she sucked in a hitching breath.

"It's okay," Erica reassured her. "Take your time."

"We-we were just kind of caught up in each other. We weren't really paying much attention to the rest of the world." Tears streamed down her cheeks, but she made no move to wipe them away.

"There's one last thing I want to ask you," Erica said, "and it might seem a little strange. Do you know the name Robert Brooks?"

"No, should I?"

"Probably not. What about the names Beatrice and Jack Gabriel?"

Sadie only seemed baffled. "No. Who are they?"

"Eighteen years ago, another couple was murdered in similar circumstances. We found DNA at the Moots' property that has a connection to this crime eighteen years ago."

Sadie's complexion paled. "You think this Robert Brooks is responsible? Was he the one who killed Grant?"

"No. He's serving a life sentence in Belmarsh Prison, so we know it wasn't him."

Erica couldn't help wondering if that meant he hadn't been responsible for the deaths eighteen years ago either. If the DNA was an exact match, she thought she'd have a good case of arguing that the same two people were responsible for both murders, and maybe even the murder of Grant and the attempted murder of Sadie, too, but since it had only been a forty-seven point five percent match, that wasn't the case.

The whole thing was infuriating.

Was this a case of a son copying a father? And if so, neither of them had ever been arrested, because they didn't have their DNA on any databases.

"And you definitely didn't know either Tabitha or Jordon Moots? Grant never mentioned them either?"

"No, I'm sorry."

Erica put away her notebook. "I'm going to let you get some rest. I think I've got everything I need, for the moment. If you remember anything else, will you give me a call or speak to the officer outside and get them to phone me?"

"Okay," she said, her voice small.

Erica paused. "I know it won't help for you to hear this, but you can't blame yourself for wanting to live. It's human instinct."

Sadie gave a tiny nod and closed her eyes.

Suddenly, they sprang open again. "Detective! My cat! Has anyone seen my cat? He's a housecat and he might have escaped during everything that happened. He's ginger and called Monty. He'll be frightened and not know what was going on."

Erica hadn't heard any reports about there being a cat, but from experience she knew that they tended to take themselves into hiding when there was a lot of activity and strange people around, and emerge later when things had quietened down.

"I'll make sure we keep an eye out for him, and I'll get someone to put some fresh food and water out for him, okay?"

"Thank you." Sadie sank back into the bed again, clearly exhausted. "He's all I've got left."

Erica took this as a sign to leave.

Sadie was going to need a lot of therapy before she was going to come out the other end of this. Not only had she gone through what she had, physically, but she also had the mental and emotional trauma of experiencing the attack. Plus, the guilt from surviving when her partner hadn't.

Erica stopped outside of the room briefly to speak with the uniformed officer positioned in the corridor. "She's our key witness, and whoever did this is going to learn that she survived the attack soon enough. There's a chance he'll want to keep her quiet. He doesn't know how much she's been able to tell us."

The bastard who'd done this was bound to be shaken by the close call. Would he retreat and go into hiding, aware the police were getting closer to catching him? Or would he decide that he had nothing to lose and that he'd kill more people while he still had the chance?

Chapter Forty-Two

His father was furious.
Liam hated it when his dad was angry. He knew to stay out of the way and was even relieved when the door was locked behind him.

Dad had warned him that the whore survived. The police could be looking for them now. She might have seen his face and given a description to the cops.

Through the locked door, Liam heard his father pace back and forth, his feet clomping, angry steps. Liam stayed huddled in the corner, his arms around his knees like he had when he was a small child, and followed the sound of his dad's footsteps.

What would they do if the police did come? Would they be arrested? What would happen to Liam? The thought terrified him. He'd never been on his own before—every memory he had contained his dad. There was no one else in his life. No other family, certainly no friends. He'd never been to school so had never had an opportunity to make any. His dad told him that was a good thing, that at school the Stacys and Chads would only laugh at him and make fun of him.

Liam thought he might have liked the chance to make friends. When he watched television or read books where groups of boys hung out and rode their bikes and had fun together, he was always filled with a strange longing, an ache in his chest, similar to how he felt when he read or saw mothers who looked as though they loved their kids.

It bothered him that the last one hadn't gone to plan. The woman had survived; it said so on the news. He wished it had been the man who'd lived instead of her, but he couldn't change things now.

He would continue to watch the news so he could find out what happened. He was glad his dad had put a television in his room, so at least he had that to keep him entertained.

Liam had no idea how long he'd be in here for until his father came to him again.

Chapter Forty-Three

Back in the office, Erica brought her boss up to speed with everything they'd learned so far, including the possible ties of the murders with the incel movement.

"Are you able to speak to the press?" he asked. "Our guy's gone home sick, and we need to give them something."

She thought about how she'd been under the weather lately. There must be something going around.

"Of course."

"Thanks. They're braying like hounds after blood out there."

It wasn't Erica's most favourite thing, but she'd do what was necessary. "When do you need me to give a statement?"

"As soon as you can. The public needs to know that we're on top of this."

She nodded. "Got it."

The national press had gathered around the front of the station, waiting for the statement to the media about the latest attack.

Erica stood in front of them, her shoulders back, her hands folded primly in front of her body. "As I'm sure you're all aware, an investigation has been launched after the body of a man, and a gravely injured woman, were discovered in Bow in the early hours of the morning. We currently believe this new attack to be linked to the murders of Tabitha and Jordon Moots last week."

A ripple of a combination of excitement and unease went through the crowd. Flashes half blinded her as photographers took pictures.

She inhaled slowly and continued. "We also believe the murders may be connected to the incel movement. The perpetrator, or possibly perpetrators, is most likely white, male, below the age of thirty, and is harbouring a hatred of women. We appeal to the public to get in touch if someone you know has given you any reason to suspect them as being the person responsible."

She took some questions from the press and answered them the best she could.

"That's all for now," she finished and turned to go back inside.

She was immediately surrounded by people, all shouting questions at her and shoving their microphones and cameras in her face. She lifted her hands to hold them off and managed to get back into the building.

It was getting late, and she'd been awake since the early hours. While she hated going home when the killer was still at large, she needed to get some sleep.

"We should call it a day," she told Shawn. "We need to rest, or we won't be any good to anyone."

"How's Poppy?" he asked. "Have you spoken to her today?"

"Yeah, she's fine. Natasha's going to drop her off after I let her know we're home."

"Okay," he said. "I'll head off now, so I'll be back within half an hour, if you want to tell Tasha it's okay to bring her home then."

"Thanks, Shawn. I appreciate it."

An hour later, she left the office to discover the press still hadn't dispersed. They spotted her immediately, and as she headed to her car, she found herself surrounded once more. They jostled and crowded her, shouting out more questions. Cameras flashed, blinding her.

Erica ducked her head and kept going. There was no point in getting herself involved in a shouting match with them.

Someone bumped her, and she lost her grip on her bag. It hit the ground, the contents spilling everywhere.

"Shit." She ducked down, picking everything back up again.

A couple of the reporters tried to help her.

"Leave it," she snapped.

It had been a long day, and she didn't need this kind of crap. Why couldn't they just be grateful for the information she had given them instead of always trying to push for more?

Damn vultures.

All she wanted was to be at home with her family and try to forget all the wickedness in the world, at least for a few hours.

Chapter Forty-Four

He'd watched her give the press conference.

She was so beautiful, but not in that trashy, fake way so many women seemed to prefer these days.

He'd seen her with her partner, too, another Chad. The partner might not be as traditionally attractive, but he was tall, with a strong physique. He'd watched the tiny moments pass between them, the brush of their hands, the secret exchange of smiles. The touch of his fingers to her lower back. The way he'd leaned in a fraction too close to speak to her.

They touched too often for people who were purely colleagues.

This woman was even worse than the rest of them because she actually believed she had power over men. She used the law—laws that were designed by men—to act as though she was better than them. To actually have the nerve to arrest them and try to get them locked up.

She was searching for him. Hunting him. He knew that.

But what if he got to her first?

It would be a key battle won in this war. Show those bitches exactly who they were dealing with. She wouldn't be acting so high and mighty when he was shining a torch into her eyes at three a.m., and he had her boyfriend hogtied and balancing a glass on his back.

No, she'd be crying and begging, and acting like the stupid little bitch she was.

He took great pleasure from his role in all of this.

He especially loved spending time in their homes while they were at work.

The couple with the dog had taken time. The first few occasions he'd gone over there, it wasn't pleased to see him. Once the animal realised he had pieces of raw steak with him, however, it quickly changed its tune. Most owners believed their dog would protect them if someone broke into their home. They convinced themselves their dog's loyalty would overcome everything else. But the reality was that dogs got scared, too, and would more than likely just run away if something frightening was happening. They were so easily bribed, as he'd quickly discovered, and they had good memories. The Moots' dog soon associated him with the treats of raw beef, and it didn't take long before the creature was pleased to see him. It would follow him all around the flat as he made himself at home, putting his feet up on the sofa, using the bathroom, helping himself to food and drink from the kitchen, even lying down in their bed. Before long, he'd almost started to think of the place as his own.

He was always careful, though. He always wore the protective suits, and it was important that he wasn't seen. He couldn't have one of the neighbours asking who the man was going into their home. He had a cover story, of course. He would tell them he was a locksmith, and he was doing some work for the owners of the flat. It wasn't a complete lie. But he was also relying on London being London. This wasn't a place where neighbours got involved in each other's businesses. Most had probably not even had a full conversation with the neighbour, most likely didn't know each other's names. The only contact they'd had was taking in the occasional parcel.

People would tell themselves it was none of their business, and they'd stick to that story right up until the point where those same neighbours were found stabbed to death in their beds.

Chapter Forty-Five

Erica woke, her heart pounding.

Something had woken her. Was it Poppy? Had her daughter cried out in her sleep from a nightmare? Or was she ill and had gone to the bathroom, and that's what had woken her? Erica was glad Poppy was old enough to get to the bathroom on time when she needed to be sick, rather than vomit all over her bed, or the floor, or herself, but Erica still didn't like the idea of her daughter having to deal with throwing up all by herself.

A warm hand on her arm made her jump.

"Everything all right?" Shawn's voice was thick with sleep.

"Yeah, I think so. Something woke me."

"Is Poppy all right?"

She loved that his first thought was of Poppy, too.

She swung her legs out of bed. "Maybe. I'll go and check."

"Let me go."

"No, it's fine. I can."

Bare feet on the soft carpet, she padded out of the bedroom and crossed the hall. Poppy didn't have a night light anymore—though she'd slept with a light on for the first few nights after the caving accident, not wanting to be trapped in the dark—but they left the hallway light on for her, and the bedroom door was always open.

She could make out Poppy's form huddled beneath the blankets.

Her daughter was fine.

She let out a breath. Everything was okay. There was no reason to get paranoid. She must have had a bad dream, and that was what had woken her.

A click came from downstairs.

Erica froze, the air trapped in her lungs. Her feet felt glued to the floor.

She'd lived in this house long enough to recognise the sound of the front door unlocking.

Someone had come into the house.

Her heartbeat pounded in her ears. She opened her mouth to call out to Shawn and then closed it again. If she spoke, whoever had broken in would know she was awake and she'd lose the element of surprise.

On tiptoes, moving as silently as possible, she slipped back into the bedroom. She hated leaving Poppy alone when there was someone else in the house, but she didn't want to risk waking her and losing this brief moment of advantage. Her phone was on the bedside table, charging. She needed to call nine-nine-nine and get a response car out here asap.

She shook Shawn's shoulder but put her hand across his mouth so he didn't speak.

Like most police officers, he was fully awake and alert within seconds. He opened his mouth, and she frowned and shook her head, then took her hand off his mouth and placed her finger to her lips. She pointed downstairs. The light coming in from the open doorway was enough for him to see her lips move: *There's someone downstairs.*

His eyes widened.

She picked up her phone and called nine-nine-nine. Keeping her voice as low as possible, still not wanting to be

THE NIGHT PROWLER 231

heard, she waited for the call operator to ask her which service she needed.

"Police," she whispered.

"One minute please. Putting you through now."

"My name is DI Erica Swift from the Met Police, and I have an intruder in my home. I need officers here immediately." She gave them her address, and the operator assured her they'd have officers with her as soon as possible.

Was that going to be quick enough?

She glanced over at Shawn who was standing at the bedroom door, leaning out so he could hear what was going on downstairs. Were they being burgled? How many of them were down there? She got the sense it was only the one, but she could be wrong about that. The two of them might be able to overpower one person, but what if there was more and they were armed? Maybe the intruder had people outside who would come to their aid?

The most important thing was keeping her family safe. Right now, she didn't give a damn if they apprehended whoever had broken into her home. All she wanted was for her loved ones to come out of this unscathed.

Shawn picked up the baton from where he'd left his belt kit beside the bed and mouthed to her: *I'm going downstairs.*

She shook her head and hissed, "No. Wait for backup to get here."

"I'm not having this person coming up here. Not with Poppy asleep in her bedroom."

She could see he was right. If this person came up the stairs, and there was an altercation, there was no possibility she'd be able to protect Poppy from hearing and even seeing the fight.

At least if it happened on the ground floor, they could go some way to protecting her from it.

She hated to think of Poppy being frightened in her own home. For her to be traumatised and scared to sleep at night. Anger swelled in her chest at the idea.

She wasn't going to let him go alone. "I'm coming with you."

He shook his head. "Stay with Poppy."

She opened her mouth to protest and then shut it again. While she didn't want to let him go alone, she didn't want to leave her daughter unprotected either. Poppy had no idea what was happening, and if this person got past Shawn, she needed to be between him and her child.

She squeezed his hand, their eye contact saying as much as their mouths ever could, and then she let him go.

Chapter Forty-Six

Shawn tightened his grip around the handle of the baton and lifted it to shoulder height, ready to take a swing at this son of a bitch's head the first opportunity he got.

All of his protective nature rose inside him. There was no chance he was going to let this person get to either Erica or Poppy. While he knew Erica was capable of looking after herself at work, this was her home, and right now she wasn't so much a detective as she was a mother.

He'd been in this house often enough that he knew where every step creaked. He was bare-footed and stepped carefully, not wanting to alert the intruder to his presence. He wasn't exactly a small person, though, and despite his best efforts, the stairs groaned.

Shawn froze.

Where was the intruder now? What were they doing? Had they broken into this home knowing it belonged to a detective? Were they here for Erica? Or had they just seen an opportunity of some kind and gone for it, unaware there were two police officers inside the property?

A swath of torchlight lit up the hallway at the bottom of the stairs. It was coming from the kitchen.

He caught a glimpse of white plastic, a hood of the same material covering the top of the person's head. A disposable coverall.

What the fuck?

The person took another step closer.

Shawn swung the baton, his teeth gritted, his muscles tense.

But they must have sensed the blow coming, as they jerked backwards at the last minute, so the baton glanced off their shoulder.

"Stop! Police!" Shawn yelled.

The intruder ran for the front door, throwing it open.

The front door hadn't been properly shut. It had been on the catch. Had they left it that way, or had this person just let themselves into their house through the front door?

There wasn't time to think about that now. The intruder ran, and Shawn took off after him. In the disposable coverall, the person was easy to see—white in the dark. He didn't want to let them get away. Shawn was bare-footed and only wearing a pair of boxer shorts and a t-shirt. He was barely aware of his lack of clothing, but the lack of footwear was more of a problem.

As he ran, he slammed his foot down on something sharp. It sliced open his sole, and he let out a yell of pain and hopped on one leg. "Fuck!"

That split second was all it had taken for the intruder to widen their lead.

Shawn tried to put his foot down again so he could run, but the pavement was slick with his own blood. Whatever he'd stood on—most likely glass—had cut him badly enough that he was going to need stitches.

His breath heaved in and out of his chest, and he forced himself to stop. He knew he was beaten.

Fuck, fuck, fuck.

He punched out at the air in frustration.

He was also aware he'd left the front door standing wide open, with Erica and Poppy terrified upstairs and not knowing what had happened to him. He hated going back to tell them the person had got away, but he didn't have much choice.

Where the hell was that patrol car? They could have been murdered in their beds by now. He'd hoped they would have arrived quicker, knowing it was other officers in danger, but then it had only been a matter of minutes since Erica had woken him to tell him someone else was in the house.

Shawn limped back, and Erica met him in the doorway.

"Are you okay?" she asked. "What happened?"

Her gaze drifted past him to land on the pavement behind him. Her eyes widened at the bloodied footprints he'd left behind.

"Oh my God. You're hurt."

"I'm fine, it's nothing. I stood on some glass, I think. How's Poppy?"

"She's fine. Still asleep. She won't know that anything happened."

"Good."

"Did you see who it was? Did you get a look at them?"

He shook his head. "They were wearing a plastic white coverall, like we might wear at a crime scene."

"Jesus Christ. He had a torch, too. At the hospital, Sadie Douglas said she'd been woken by a torch being shone in her eyes."

"It's dark, Erica," Shawn said. "Most people who break into homes would probably bring a torch. It doesn't mean it's the same person."

"And the white boilersuit?" she pressed. "She said the person who attacked her wore one, too."

He opened his mouth to reassure her that it didn't mean it was the same person and shut it again. He was trying to make her feel better as her partner, but now he needed to switch his brain to police work. If anyone else had been saying the same thing to him, he'd be joining the dots.

"I didn't see a knife," he said instead.

"What did he want, Shawn? Who is he?"

"I wish I knew."

Sirens came in the distance, and the sky lit up with flashing blue lights. Backup was finally here.

Erica helped him into the kitchen and sat him in one of the chairs. She handed him a tea towel. "Put some pressure on it. I'm going to go out and meet the response unit, fill them in on everything that's happened."

Shawn did as she said, listening to the muffled voices from outside.

After only a matter of minutes, Erica returned with two impossibly young-looking police constables with her.

Her gaze dropped to his foot. "You need to get to hospital, get that cut seen to."

"I'm fine," he insisted.

Erica raised her eyebrows. "You're bleeding all over the floor. You're definitely not fine."

He glanced down at the tea towel wrapped around his foot. Sure enough, it was already saturated, and there were blood spots on the laminate. "Shit. Okay, fine, but you keep someone with you until I get back."

"Don't worry," one of the officers said, "we'll get statements and get forensics in here, too. If this was the person we think it might be..."

He didn't need to finish the rest of the sentence. If this person was the killer, they might have left prints around.

"How did he open the front door?" Erica said.

Shawn remembered what he'd seen. "I think he just let himself in. Wasn't that what it looked like with the other victims' houses, too? Like he'd just walked right in? No sign of a break-in?"

Erica suddenly went to her handbag and rifled through it, then went to her jacket and checked the pockets.

"What it is?" Shawn asked.

"I think I've lost my keys. Or maybe someone stole them. They must have used them to get into the house."

"What? Didn't you have them when you got home last night?"

She shook her head. "No, you were already home, remember. I didn't use them then."

Chapter Forty-Seven

The memory of dropping her bag and being surrounded by reporters filled Erica's head. Had someone stolen them then? Had one of the people she'd assumed was from the press actually been someone else entirely?

Something clicked.

Tabitha Moots had lost her keys, too. What about Sadie Douglas? Had she also lost her keys sometime before the attack? Is that how this bastard got in?

He had a key to their homes.

It was already starting to get light.

"I need to talk to Sadie Douglas, find out if she lost her keys recently, and if so, what locksmith she used to replace them."

It was too early to be waking up a hospital patient, but Erica didn't think they had much choice. Besides, she needed to take Shawn there to get his foot stitched up. She was sure Sadie wouldn't mind being woken if it meant catching the person who'd murdered Grant.

She got dressed and woke up Poppy and took her to her sister's house, full of apologies, then drove to the hospital. She left Shawn in Accident and Emergency and then made her way up to Sadie's ward.

The hospital was waking up now, doctors and nurses doing their rounds, staff bringing breakfast trays to the patients.

She was relieved to find Sadie already awake. She was sitting up in bed, and her eyes widened upon seeing the detective standing at the door.

"You're here early."

"I know. I'm sorry, but I need to ask you some more questions. It's important. Did you or Grant ever lose your house keys?"

Sadie nodded. "It's how I met Grant," she said. "I'd lost my keys, and I couldn't get in my car or my flat. He helped me break in."

Erica arched an eyebrow. "He helped you break in?"

Sadie risked a tiny smile. "Not like that. He was helping me, honestly. There were no bad intentions, I'm sure."

"So did you have a new key cut?"

Sadie shook her head. "No, I had to get a whole new lock. I was stupid and didn't have a spare anywhere, so I didn't have much choice."

"Can you describe the person who changed your lock?"

"I'm sorry, but no, I can't. I wasn't at the flat at the time. I had to work, and Grant offered to wait in to meet the locksmith. He did, and the lock was changed, and I honestly didn't think anything more of it."

If only Grant was still alive so they could get a description from him.

"Do you think it's the same person who broke into the flat?" Sadie asked. "The same person who killed Grant?"

Erica nodded. "There's definitely a connection, yes."

She needed to get back into the office. They needed a list of everyone who worked at the locksmith's and find out if any of them fit the profile of the man they were looking for.

Erica left Sadie and swung by Accident and Emergency. She didn't have much hope that they'd have fixed Shawn up already, but, to her surprise, he was sitting waiting for her.

"I pulled the detective card," he told her. "Told them I was needed to catch a killer."

"You are," she said. "Are you okay to walk?"

"Yeah. They jabbed me with a numbing injection, so I can't feel a thing."

"Okay, just be careful not to put too much weight on it."

It was a short drive back to the office where Gibbs was already in and waiting for them. The rest of the team were in, too, and Erica could sense the worry among them all because of the break-in.

"Are you both okay?" Gibbs asked them.

"Apart from Shawn's foot, we're fine."

"Was Poppy all right?"

Erica nodded. "She didn't really understand what was going on, just that we had an emergency at work. She's used to being uprooted at all times of night and day, so it didn't seem all that strange to her."

Erica realised that Shawn being in the house in the middle of the night pretty much gave them away, but no one had mentioned it, and she certainly wasn't going to bring it up herself.

"Sadie confirmed that she'd lost her keys as well and had her lock changed. It was the same place that Tabitha used."

"There's more than one person who works at the locksmith. We can't just arrest all of them."

"We need their names, addresses, and to find out if they have any prior convictions. We believe he's male, white, and below the age of thirty."

The office grew loud and busy with the clacking of fingers on computer keys and the ringing of phones and people talking.

A flash of a face came to her. Not the person she'd spoken to, but the man who'd slipped into the back of the shop. The one the other employee had said wasn't the sharpest tool in the box.

She couldn't recall ever receiving the shop rota. God dammit. They'd dropped the ball on that—something that could have cost her and her family's lives.

Hannah shouted over from her desk, "We've got one person who works there who matches that description. His name is Liam Coulter. He's twenty-nine years old. He lives at an address in Bromley."

"Where is he likely to be?"

Erica checked the time. The hours had flown by since she'd first been woken by the intruder. It was just gone nine a.m. now.

"I assume he's at work."

"We'll arrest him there then. Let's get a team together."

Chapter Forty-Eight

Erica and Shawn entered the shop, garnering attention from the few customers in there and the older man behind the counter.

Erica held up her ID. "We're looking for Liam Coulter. Is he here?"

The other man nodded. "Yeah, he's just over—"

A flash of movement came from the back of the shop. A young man pushed over a stand containing keychains that had different names on them. They hit the floor with a crash and a jangle.

The man vanished out of the exit leading to the rear of the shop, the door swinging shut behind him.

"He's on the move!" Erica spoke into her radio.

Aware this might happen, they had already positioned uniformed officers around the building. Was Liam going to be armed? Unlikely, considering the setting. She couldn't imagine him bringing a blade to work, but it was still important to be cautious. They all wore stab proof vests for protection.

They followed Liam out of the back to find one of the uniformed officers already on him, pinning him to the ground, putting cuffs on his wrists.

Liam sobbed into the dirt. "I'm sorry, I'm sorry. It wasn't my fault. I couldn't stop him."

The son of a bitch was crying? Seriously?

Erica's heart grew hard.

"Liam Coulter. You are under arrest for the murders of Tabitha and Jordon Moots, the murder of Grant Cipri, and the rape and attempted murder of Sadie Douglas. You do not have to say anything—"

Her voice was drowned out by the increasingly louder sobs coming from Liam.

The arresting officer glanced up at her and shook his head. She understood what he was saying. It was a shake of disgust and dismay. Liam's shoulders shook as he cried like a child.

He wasn't crying for all the people he'd hurt, the lives he'd destroyed. He was crying because he'd got caught.

Erica had read the sort of vitriol people like him spouted against women. So what? He was feeling sorry for himself? Again, because he hadn't won some imagined genetic lottery. There were few times in her life where she'd felt utter repulsion for a person, and she felt that way about him right now.

They got him down to the station and into one of the interview rooms.

"I can take it from here, boss," Hannah said. "It's what we're trained to do. You've had a long night. Take a break."

Erica normally liked to sit in on interviews, or at least watch them remotely, but she was exhausted and did want a break.

"Okay, thanks, Hannah."

She needed coffee, but the thought turned her stomach. Maybe she'd have a cup of tea for once. Her exhaustion travelled right down to the bone. She considered closing her eyes for a moment. No one would judge her for it.

Half an hour later, as Erica sat dozing at her desk, Hannah came to find her.

"Something's not quite right."

Erica woke herself fully. "What do you mean?"

"You need to speak to him yourself. I don't know if the whole thing is an act, but he says he hasn't hurt anyone. That it's his father who is responsible. There's something about the way he talks, too. I don't know why, but I feel like I'm talking to a much younger person."

"Younger? How much younger?"

Hannah grimaced. "Like a child."

"You can't be serious?"

"He insists he didn't do anything. That it was all his dad."

"That's bullshit. We have his DNA at the scene. It's a match."

They'd put a rush on it as soon as he'd been booked.

"I know that," Hannah said, "but he says everything is down to his father."

Erica thought of something.

"Wait a minute. He could be telling the truth. What about the old case, the one Robert Brooks is serving time for? DNA that has less than a fifty-percent match to Liam's DNA was found at that scene. Liam must have only been, what? Eleven or twelve years old at the time of that murder? That DNA most likely belongs to his father."

Hannah's eyes grew round. "So his father *is* the one responsible?"

"Or they're killing people together." Erica rubbed her hand across her mouth. "Which also means that Robert Brooks is innocent of murdering Beatrice and Jack Gabriel."

"Holy shit. Is this enough proof to get him freed?"

"I'd say that it's certainly enough to create reasonable doubt that Robert was responsible, and if we can get Liam to go on record that his father murdered the Gabriels eighteen years ago, then there will be no way Robert will stay locked up."

Hannah shook her head. "That poor bloke. Almost his whole life behind bars for a murder he didn't commit. I think I would have lost my mind."

"We need to find the father. Do we know who he is yet?"

"His name is Liam as well."

Erica had to resist rolling her eyes. "Well, that's convenient."

"We have a driver's licence for him, though it expired eleven years ago. He's registered as living at the same address as Liam Junior."

"We need to get around there. Something about this isn't adding up."

Her head was spinning. Did they really have the wrong man? Everything told her that they didn't, but something was off.

Chapter Forty-Nine

It didn't take long for Erica to put a team together and get to the address in Bromley.

She also made sure the rest of the force knew Liam Coulter Senior was a person of interest. If he'd got word that his son had been arrested at work, it might have spooked him, and he could have decided to go on the run.

Which one of them had been in her house last night? Had it been the father or son? Or perhaps it was neither and was someone else entirely? Shawn had reported that he'd believed it to have been a younger man, but he'd never actually seen their face. Liam Senior could just keep himself fit.

What had Liam Senior been doing all this time? Why had he been living under the radar? Some people did—they lived as off grid as possible—but this was East London. For the most part, the only people who did that were homeless. Was it because of his penchant for killing that he'd kept his head down? Maybe the case where Robert Brooks had been convicted had frightened him off, and it had taken him eighteen years to regain his confidence and kill again, only this time with his son at his side.

The Coulter house was tired and unloved. White paint, that was now closer to grey, peeled from the facias. The guttering was broken and hanging off. The windows were single glazed and warped. The place must have been freezing in the winter. The front garden was no better—a mess of weeds and a tangle of brambles.

The rest of the properties in the street were tidy and well-maintained. She'd bet the neighbours hated this one. If she'd driven past, she'd have assumed it had been abandoned, which, considering the property prices in London, would have been unusual.

"Let's get around the back," she said. "Make sure he doesn't try to make a run for it."

"If the back has as many brambles as the front," Shawn commented, "I don't think he'll get very far."

Erica let one of the uniformed officers, PC Boal—a compact Asian woman with short, cropped dark hair and beautiful eyes—take the lead. She was wearing a protective stab vest, her partner right beside her.

Boal hammered on the door. "Mr Coulter? It's the police. Open the door."

No response came.

This didn't surprise Erica. "Let's get the Bosher over here."

PC Boal stepped out of the way, and another officer carrying the red battering ram took position in front of the door. The wood was so buckled and old that it only took two strikes for the lock to break open and the door to swing wide.

They moved fast, shouts of "Police," echoing through the house as several uniformed officers entered the building.

Erica and Shawn followed close behind. This was a potentially dangerous man, suspected of taking at least two lives and being involved in the murders of three more, and attempted murder, too. Some people were like rabid dogs when backed into a corner, and he could well be armed.

The interior of the property matched the exterior. Unloved, wallpaper peeling, the carpet threadbare and filthy.

"Clear," someone called from the living room.

"Kitchen's clear, too," another officer shouted.

They moved deeper into the house, going upstairs and checking the bedrooms.

"Does a child live here?" PC Boal called back to Erica.

"Not that we've been informed of," Erica replied. She stepped closer to get a better idea of what had prompted Boal to ask the question.

Unlike the rest of the house, this room appeared to be kept in good nick. The walls were freshly painted light blue. There was a shelf full of reading books and even a laptop. The bed had a duvet with footballs printed on it. The bedroom was for a child. Not a young boy, but a child nonetheless.

"Does Liam Junior have any children?" Erica asked no one in particular.

Shawn shook his head. "Not that we know of."

As well as murdering couples inside their homes, was it possible he'd also kidnapped a child?

"We need to search this place, focus on any places a child might be hiding." Erica noticed something else. "Look at this."

On the inside of the child's bedroom door were several bolt locks.

"They're on the outside, too." She peered at the locks on the outside. They were blackened with rust. She used a gloved hand to try to slide one along, but it didn't budge. The ones inside were still shiny silver—not new, perhaps, but definitely well used.

"It's been a while since these ones were locked and unlocked, but I'd say the ones on the inside are used regularly."

Shawn frowned. "I don't understand. Why have locks on the inside of a room?"

"Because whoever's room it is was trying to keep someone out?"

PC Boal leaned closer. "Someone was trying to keep Liam out?"

"Which Liam?" Shawn commented.

Something didn't quite fit.

Erica shook her head. "We need to keep questioning Liam Junior. Find out if he was keeping a child here."

Shawn picked up one of the books on the bedside table and opened it. "The inscription inside reads, 'To Junior, love Dad.'"

"This is Liam Junior's room?"

Shawn looked around. "If so, he hasn't changed it since he was a child."

"I need to see the rest of the house," she said.

Some people kept their childhood bedrooms the same, didn't they? They didn't have the inclination to bother clearing it out or redecorating. She probably wouldn't be focusing on it so much if it wasn't for the double set of locks on the doors, inside and out.

Had Liam's father locked him in here as a child? And if so, why were there newer locks on the inside?

"Detectives, you need to see this!" an officer shouted from down the hall.

Erica and Shawn exchanged a glance and then hurried in the direction they'd been called.

They stopped outside a second bedroom.

Erica stepped into the room slowly, widening her eyes, her jaw dropping. She didn't know why she was surprised at the horror around her. She'd seen so much of it recently.

She found herself in a second bedroom, almost as untouched as the first. But it was what was in the bed that drew her full attention.

A mummified corpse of what she assumed had once been a man lay in the bed. The covers had congealed to the corpse as it had decomposed, becoming a part of it, as had the mattress, so what was now essentially only a skeleton was sunken into the bed.

There was no bad smell, only a kind of musty staleness that came from a room being shut up for so long. One thing was clear, and that was Liam hadn't been sleeping in this bed. Since there were only two bedrooms, it meant the childlike one was his.

Erica didn't know which situation she found more disturbing. That Liam, as an almost thirty-year-old man, was living in a child's bedroom, or that he'd been living in this house with a decomposing body.

She stared at the body, trying to piece together what she was seeing.

"Any idea who he might be?" she asked.

"This house is registered to Liam Coulter Senior, and since he doesn't appear to be anywhere to be found, I'd say it's a good guess to assume this is him," the officer said.

"So Liam has been living in this house with his dead father? For how long?"

The officer shrugged. "It's hard to say. From the condition of the corpse, I'd say it's been years. Decades, even."

"Jesus Christ. Why didn't he report the death? Why has no one noticed?"

Her mind turned over the possibility of what Liam's life had been like. Had he still been a child when his father had died—if that was, in fact, what had happened here? Had he grown up with his father's body rotting in that bed? How had he fed himself? How had he survived?

And what about the locks on the door? Did that mean his father used to lock him in the bedroom? Why?

Had the father died from natural causes, or had Liam had something to do with it?

The possibility of Liam's father dying while Liam had been locked in that room crept into her mind. While she didn't want to feel an ounce of sympathy for the man, she saw him as a young boy, locked in his bedroom, only to find no one was coming to let him out again because his father had died in bed, and no one else even knew he existed.

"That's not all," Shawn said, turning around.

One of the walls was covered in newspaper clippings and printed-out information. Photographs of beautiful women, their eyes and mouths scratched out with black marker. News reports of other violent episodes that were put down to incels—the murders of eight people in Texas when an incel went on a shooting spree, and the murder of ten people with a van in Vancouver.

Words encouraging rape and murder, violence against women, and referring to women as sandwich makers and baby factories, were scrawled all over the walls.

Chapter Fifty

They waited for both SOCO and the pathologist to arrive. Uniformed police guarded the scene, while others went door to door, questioning the neighbours to find out if anyone had witnessed what had been going on in the house.

"How could no one have reported the smell?" Erica said, still in disbelief. "Didn't the council notice anything was wrong?"

Shawn shrugged. "I guess as long as the bills were all paid, no one had any reason to think anything was wrong."

Erica's phone rang. It was Professor Nigel Reed.

"It's not a great time, Professor," she said.

"Sorry, I won't keep you a minute."

"Go on."

"I remembered what the writing reminded me of," he said. "It was from someone who had a dissociative identity disorder. There were two sides of him that were warring against each other, and that was why his handwriting was so conflicting."

Was that what was happening here? Liam had insisted his father was responsible for the murders, but had it been Liam Junior, believing himself to be his father?

"Thank you, Professor. You may hear from me again if I need you to come to court."

"Of course. Whatever I can do to help."

Liam Senior hated women, and he'd brought his son up to hate women as well. All the online chatter encouraged him to follow in his father's footsteps, except he used the medium of his father's personality to commit the crimes. It distanced him from it. Made him believe he wasn't actually culpable for the murders of those people.

One of the uniformed officers got their attention.

"Detectives, you might want to speak to one of the neighbours across the road. She's been living in the street for forty years."

Erica nodded. "Take me to her."

A woman in her sixties stood on her doorstep, wrapped in a fluffy brown dressing gown, a pair of slippers on her feet.

"This is Mrs Miggins," the officer said. "She has information on the residents of the house."

The older woman frowned, her lips pursing. "Yes, I remember the man who used to live there. We're going back a long time, though. He wasn't a friendly person. Always had a face on him, you know, like glaring, and wouldn't meet your eye. I tried to say hello to him a couple of times, but he ignored me and kept walking. I gave up after a while. I thought maybe he had mental health issues or something or was one of those autistic people, though we didn't really have a name for it, or at least not one that was regularly used back then. Honestly, I thought he was just a bit of an arsehole."

"What about a child?" Erica asked. "Did you ever see him with a boy? His son, perhaps?"

Her rheumy blue eyes widened. "A son? No, definitely not. I never saw him with anyone. I would have remembered if he'd been with a boy, because I'd have checked up on him. I can't imagine that man would have been any kind of decent caregiver."

"Did you notice when you stopped seeing him?"

"No, sorry. Like I said, I didn't have any interaction with him. I assumed he moved."

"But no one else moved in?" Erica checked.

The woman brightened. "Oh, yes. A young man. Liam, I think his name is. He's still there now."

"How young was he when he moved in?"

"Oh God. I have no idea. I find it impossible to guess ages. Young—though everyone seems young to me these days."

Had Liam raised himself in that house, keeping himself out of view until he was old enough—or at least *looked* old enough—that people wouldn't ask questions? Had he slipped out after dark to find food? What had he done for money? Perhaps he'd had access to his father's bank card and was able to withdraw cash. If Liam had been in his teens when his father had died, then people wouldn't have bothered to ask too many questions, and he was computer literate enough to get the paperwork he needed to move forward to live what could be perceived as a normal life, at least on the surface.

Leaving the crime scene in the hands of SOCO and the uniformed officers, Erica and Shawn returned to the office. She was aware that they still had Liam Junior in custody. They had enough to charge him now, but, after seeing the house, she worried about his state of mind.

As Hannah had suggested, she needed to talk to him herself.

Back at the station, in one of the interview rooms, Liam Coulter Junior sat on the other side of the table, his wrists cuffed. He had a solicitor with him that they had provided, since he didn't have his own.

Erica ran through all the information for the interview tape, ensuring that he knew his rights.

"My name is DI Swift, Liam. I want to talk to you about the reason you've been arrested."

Liam didn't look at her but stared down at the table instead, his neck bent.

"It wasn't me," he said. "I didn't do anything. I only did what he told me."

"What are you talking about, Liam? Only did what *who* told you?"

"My dad. He's going to be so angry when he finds out I'm talking to you."

Erica glanced over to Shawn, whose eyebrows pulled down in a frown. "When was the last time you saw your dad, Liam?"

"What do you mean? I saw him this morning." His mouth twisted. "At least, I think it was this morning."

Was he talking about seeing his body still lying in the bed, or did he mean something else? They didn't have any physical proof yet that the body found in the bed was Liam's father, but Erica was already convinced.

"Liam," she spoke carefully. Why did she feel as though she was talking to a child, when this was a grown man sitting across the table from her? Not only a grown man, but a man who was capable of rape and murder. "When was the last time you spoke to your father?"

"Today. I speak to him every day."

"Do you understand that your father has been dead for many years?"

He huffed air out of his nose. "No, he hasn't. You must have him confused with someone else."

They were doing DNA tests on the corpse as fast as they could, but Erica really needed that solid proof. She also wondered if the DNA would match that taken from the Gabriel crime scene—the sample that had previously been unidentified, but that had just short of a fifty-percent match to Liam's.

She pushed photographs of Tabitha and Jordon across the table.

"Do you recognise these people?"

He stared at the photographs for a long time. Tears streamed down his cheeks, and he palmed them away and nodded. "Yes."

"Where do you know them from?"

He shook his head. "I can't say. My dad will be angry."

"Your dad won't be angry, Liam. Your dad is dead."

His head snapped up, eyes wide. "No. You're lying."

"I promise you I'm not lying. He's been dead for a very long time." Erica remembered what the professor, and Jasmin, and Hannah had said about being childlike, and asked, "How old are you, Liam?

His gaze darted from side to side. "Twelve."

"Do you know what year it is?"

"No. I don't think so."

"Do you go to school?

He pinched his lips together. "My dad homeschools me. I'm good with books."

"Your dad is dead, Liam," she repeated. "He can't have been homeschooling you, because he died a very long time ago."

He put his hands over his ears. "Stop it, stop it."

"Maybe we should take a break," the solicitor said.

For once, she agreed with him.

"Okay. Can I get you something to eat or drink, Liam?"

"A hot chocolate," Liam said.

"Coming right up."

While she went to get the drink from the machine, a message came up on her phone.

DNA taken from the remains is a 47.5% match to Liam Coulter Junior. The corpse found in the house is Liam's father. It also matches the DNA taken from the Gabriels' crime scene.

Erica paused and let the magnitude of this information sink in. This was proof that Liam's father had been present at the murders Robert Brooks had been convicted of eighteen years ago. It was enough to cause probable doubt and would most likely make him a free man.

It also meant that Liam still believed his father to be alive.

The absolute horror of what Liam must have gone through as a child gradually sank into Erica's soul. Why hadn't he gone for help when he'd realised his father was dead? Was there no one who could have checked on him?

Shawn joined her at the machine, and she filled him in on what she'd learned.

"What the hell are we going to do with him?" Shawn asked. "Is he acting? Is this all just a ploy to get himself into a mental hospital rather than spend the rest of his life in prison?"

"Mental hospitals aren't exactly pleasant places to be," Erica said.

"Maybe not, but they're better than prison."

Erica raised her eyebrows. "I think that's a matter of opinion. Anyway, we're going to have to get psych down here for an assessment, try to figure out if he's faking this whole thing."

"If he's faking, I think he should have considered a life on the stage instead of a life of rape and murder. He'd have won an Oscar."

"One thing we can be sure of is that he must have had one fucked-up childhood. His father was a murderer who let Robert Brooks take the fall. He kept Liam away from the rest of society and fed him poisonous ideas about women."

"Do you think Liam Junior might have been there when the Gabriels were killed? Did he take Liam with him?"

Erica blew out a breath. "I have no idea, and I'm not even sure Liam would know either. If he can't tell the difference between when he's his father and when he's a boy, how's he going to know if it was his father actually committing a crime eighteen years ago, or if it's a crime he's committed recently *as* his father. When he's at work, or in public, he's his father. But when he comes home, he becomes twelve-year-old Liam again. The locks on the bedroom...." She shook her head, trying to piece everything together. "Who has he been trying to keep out? His imaginary father?"

"I don't think he's been trying to keep him out. I think he's been locking himself in, except in his mind, it's his father who's been locking him in, just like he did when Liam was a child."

"Liam Junior is also insisting that he never hurt anyone. That it's his father who does it. I heard from Hannah that he claims he was just made to help clean up and keep a lookout."

Shawn rubbed his hand across his lips. "What are we saying here, that he thinks he's his father?"

"I think we might be dealing with some kind of split personality, maybe, or dissociative identity disorder. His father kept him locked inside that room when he was a child, and then when his father died and he no longer had that heavy hand hanging over him, instead of trying to branch out on his own, he somehow absorbed his father's personality. Perhaps the grief was too much for him and he snapped. When he's in his twelve-year-old identity, his father is still alive."

It frightened her that she'd been on this man's radar. Not just her but Shawn, as well, and if he'd been in the house with them both, then maybe he'd have hurt Poppy, too.

The idea sickened her.

"He's a deeply traumatised man."

"There's still a chance he's faking it," Shawn reminded her.

She took the drink from the dispenser. "Let's get back in there."

She carried the hot chocolate back into the interview room and placed it on the table in front of Liam.

Liam sat, not making eye contact with any of them. His head lowered. He chewed on his lower lip, his knee bouncing under the table.

"Are you okay, Liam?"

He pouted and shrugged.

"How's your drink?" she asked, nodding at the hot chocolate he'd requested.

Liam picked up the cup and took a sip. "Good," he muttered.

Erica angled her head, noting what hand he was holding the cup in. "What hand do you use to write with, Liam?"

"My left," he said. "I've always used my left."

Erica remembered one of the things she'd been told during the postmortems, how the angle of the blade and the position of the puncture wounds indicated that the person who'd held the knife had been right-handed.

"And what about your dad?" she asked. "What did he write with?"

"He uses his right hand," Liam said. "He never likes that I use my left. He tried to teach me how to write with my other hand for a while, hitting my knuckles with a wooden ruler if I didn't do what he wanted. But it never worked. I still always use my left."

Was that enough to prove that it hadn't been the younger version of Liam who'd been mentally present when the victims had been killed, but instead the adult version who he'd somehow convinced himself was his father? It didn't make him innocent, but it might keep him out of prison and get him a place in a psychiatric unit for the criminally insane instead.

Erica thought Liam truly believed it was his father who had raped and murdered. Maybe he hadn't been able to come to terms with his own desires and so had used the 'father' version of himself to do the grisly tasks.

Liam must have witnessed the murders of Beatrice and Jack Gabriel. Had that been the moment his mind had snapped, or had it been later, after he'd found his father dead in bed?

"Did you leave those messages for us, Liam?" she asked. "The ones written on the walls?"

He sniffed and nodded. "I didn't want everyone to think I was completely bad. I knew what he was doing was wrong."

"Why couldn't you stop him?"

"I just couldn't," he replied.

"Why not?"

His voice grew louder. "I couldn't!"

"Explain to me—"

"I'm not talking to you anymore. I'll talk to him," he nodded over at Shawn, "but not you."

"Why won't you talk to me, Liam?"

He pressed his lips into a line but didn't respond.

"Is it because I'm a woman?"

"You're evil. You're out to ruin men. You want to make it so men are the inferior sex, so you can walk all over us." A flash of anger appeared in his eyes.

Her blood ran cold. Something about him had changed, the angle of his jaw, the tendons in his throat flexing. Was this the man hidden beneath the boy? The same one who'd raped and murdered his victims?

Shawn opened his mouth to stand up for her, but she held up her hand to stop him. There was no point arguing. From what she could tell, this was how Liam had been raised. It had been indoctrinated in him since he'd been a small child. A few exchanged words in an interview room weren't going to make any difference.

"What does your dad do for a living?" she asked.

"He's a locksmith. Why?"

"Did he ever teach you how to do his job?"

He shrugged. "Sure. He teaches me everything."

Had that been enough for Liam to pass as a regular person when he'd been at work? Had he believed he was his father whenever he was outside of the house, or with other adults, or during the times when he had the urge to rape and kill? But when he was at home, or in a situation where it was safer for him to be that child instead of a man who needed to take responsibility, Liam reverted back to being the same age he'd been when his father had died.

That was what the words written on the wall had been about.

The boy version of Liam had been trying to reach through, to stop the part of him that became his father and wanted to kill. The two sides of him had somehow existed at the same time.

Liam was a monster, but he was that way because his monster of a father had created him.

Chapter Fifty-One

Though they'd stopped the man responsible for killing three people and attempting to kill a fourth, and they'd freed an innocent man from prison, Erica couldn't shake the weight that sat heavy on her heart.

Robert Brooks no longer had the rest of his life behind bars ahead of him, but he'd already lost so much. Almost the whole of his adult life had been spent locked up. He'd missed his prime time to marry and have a family, and while he wasn't old now, and perhaps that would still be in his future, he had to figure out how to adjust to a normal life. The damage that would have been done to him over the past eighteen years inside wasn't something he'd just get over. He'd be institutionalised and have no idea how to function back in the real world. Plus, there was the stigma of having been convicted of murdering two people in their beds. Yes, his name might have been cleared, but there would always be those who wouldn't believe he was innocent. People would still whisper behind his back and wonder if he had actually done it. No smoke without a fire and all that.

Nothing would ever get those eighteen years back again. The damage had already been done. Mistakes shouldn't have been made in the first place.

Robert Brooks wasn't the only thing that was bothering her. Everything about this case had left her heart-sick. She wasn't a sheltered person by any means, but the hate and vitriol that existed out there against innocent young women made her both furious and sickened.

This was the world her daughter was growing up in. Before she knew it, Poppy would be a teenager, and then what? Would some teenage boy set his sights on her, and if she dared to reject him, would he start posting online that she was a whore and a slut and how she deserved to be raped and killed, all because she wasn't interested?

Would Poppy's life one day be in danger because she dared to say no?

Erica honestly didn't know what to do with the barrage of emotions just the thought of it stirred inside her.

Erica went to Gibbs' office to let him know they'd closed the case.

"Good work, Detective," he told her.

"Is it?"

"You and your team got a dangerous man off the street. I'd say that was excellent work."

"One." She held up a finger to demonstrate her point. "One person. That's all we took off the streets. How many more of these bastards are out there? Thousands, if not tens of thousands, maybe even hundreds of thousands. It's like a fucking epidemic."

"They're not all killers, Erica."

"Today they might not be, but what's it going to take to push another one over the edge? Is some teenage girl going to snub one of these boy's advances, so he decides to kill her? Snuff out her life because he can't handle rejection and believes he should be entitled to have whatever he wants?"

He nodded. "Most likely, yes, that's going to happen."

She shook her head in dismay. "It's the utter selfishness of it, that they think they deserve to destroy people's lives just because they're too ugly, both physically and mentally, to get laid. And then they expect sympathy? They expect people to feel sorry for them 'cause no one understands them? Maybe if they weren't so fucking pathetic, they'd be able to get a girlfriend, but no, it's never going to be a problem with them, is it?"

With every word, she got angrier and angrier.

"It's not all men," he said.

"No, I know it's not. There are good men around, like you and Shawn, and the kind of man my father was when he was alive. But the trouble is that it's *enough* men. It's enough men that women don't feel safe. Enough that some women believe they should just let men take what they want rather than them pay the ultimate price." She tutted her tongue against the roof of her mouth. "What was it Margaret Atwood said? Men are afraid women will laugh at them, but women are afraid men will kill them. That's the truth of this situation. All it takes is for a woman to make a man look stupid and they risk losing their life for it. The whole thing is fucking disgusting."

Gibbs sucked in a deep breath. "They say these young men have mental health issues of their own, that they're isolated and depressed and suffering from anxiety. They have a huge fear of rejection, and they can't connect with people, mainly because they have a history of being rejected by their primary caregiver when they were younger."

Unaccustomed fury rose inside her. "Let me guess, by their 'primary caregiver' the studies are talking about their mothers?"

He shrugged. "They just say primary caregiver."

She pursed her lips and shook her head. "See, this is the problem. Women get the blame for everything. These young men hate women because they won't sleep with them, and instead of looking at themselves and thinking maybe they could do something to work on themselves, they call for women and girls to be raped and murdered. And now we're going even further back, and now, as well as blaming the women for not wanting to sleep with them, we blame the mothers for not raising them right."

"It was the father in the case of Liam, Erica. No one is blaming the mother."

"No? 'Cause it sure as hell sounds to me like these studies are. At what point are we simply going to point the finger at the men and boys themselves and ask them to take responsibility for their own feelings and actions? Women and girls are raised by these same parents, and you don't see them going around raping and murdering boys? These young men are growing up believing that they're entitled to have it all, just because they're male, and the internet is giving them a place to have those thoughts confirmed. It's fucking toxic."

She was breathing hard, her fists bunched. She was one breath away from saying that they should be strung up and made an example of but managed to stop herself.

What good would it do?

She pushed her hands into her eyes. "I'm sorry. I'm just so angry and frustrated about it all. It feels like I'm fighting a losing battle. Nothing is ever going to change."

"With strong, clever women like you around, they will," he reassured her.

"I wish that was true. Maybe if I had a son, I'd feel like I could do something to change things, to make sure he grows up right, but I don't."

"No, but you're an inspiration to your daughter, and you're keeping the streets safe for her."

She pressed her lips together. "Am I, though?"

"Without women like you, the world would be a much uglier place."

She didn't want to feel like it was an 'us against them' situation.

"Look," Gibbs continued, "you're upset. I get it. Why don't you let Shawn drive you home."

"I'm capable of driving myself home, sir."

"Well, since you're both going in that direction anyway..."

He let the words trail off. Of course he knew. How could he not? A police report had been done when the break-in had happened. They'd both been at Erica's address in the middle of the night. What else would have been going on?

Erica opened her mouth, but he raised a hand.

"I don't need to know what's going on in your private business."

It was his way of telling her he was looking in the opposite direction.

"Thanks, sir."

"I'm sure I don't need to tell you to keep it out of the office, too."

"No, sir, you don't."

He smiled. "Good. Well, that's that, then."

She got to her feet. "Thank you, sir."

He'd given her a gift of sorts. A way of telling her not to worry, or at least worry a little less about that one thing.

When so much of the world was in turmoil, he was offering her that small amount of peace.

Chapter Fifty-Two

Erica took a breath and hit the buzzer for the correct flat. She waited for a moment, until a voice said, "Yes?"

She leaned in slightly. "It's Erica Swift."

"Come on up."

The high-rise flats weren't exactly pretty, but after where he'd been living for the past eighteen years, she'd bet they felt like luxury.

She caught a lift up to the ninth floor and walked down the corridor in the direction the plaque on the wall indicated.

He was waiting at the front door.

It was strange to see him in normal clothes and not behind bars.

"Mr Brooks," she said. "Good to see you."

"Call me Robert, please. Come inside. Can I make you a cup of tea?"

"Coffee, if you've got it," she said.

"It's only instant."

"Instant is pretty much all I drink."

She followed him into the small kitchen. The flat was compact but clean. It was also noticeably bare. It was clear a life hadn't been lived here. There were no framed photographs on the walls or nicknacks that had been collected during a family holiday. The front of the fridge was clear of a child's drawings or fridge magnets.

Erica tried not to feel sad for him and failed. What an absolute waste his life in prison had been. She couldn't even imagine how he must be feeling. Robbed of his freedom for eighteen years. Accused and convicted of murdering a woman who he'd actually loved. How had he not lost his mind?

He boiled the kettle and made them both coffee, then gestured for them to take it into the living room.

"Sorry about the state of the sofa," he said. "Everything you see in here are donations from a charity. I'll be compensated, financially, probably enough to buy a place of my own and fill it with expensive furniture, but nothing is going to bring back those years."

"I'm so sorry."

"It's not your fault. You were the one who finally proved my innocence."

"The police failed you. The solicitors failed you. The system failed you, and I'm part of that system, so please let me apologise. I know it's nowhere near enough, but it's all I have."

He wrapped his hands around his mug and lowered his head. "Thank you."

"How are you finding things?" she asked.

"Not great." He shrugged. "It's strange, isn't it, how when you're inside, you dream of freedom. But now I've actually got it, I'm not sure I even want it. I'm lonely, though my sister has visited, and overwhelmed a lot of the time. Honestly, I kind of miss prison. There are too many choices out here. Little things, like trying to decide what to make for a meal, feel like too much. Have you been to a supermarket lately? Those places are insane. How many different choices of pasta sauce does one person need? I don't even like being able to decide what time to go to bed and then get up again. I'm still setting my alarm for the same time I had to get up when I was inside. I haven't had a lie-in for eighteen years and I can't see myself having one now."

"What about a job? Any ideas on that front?"

"The people from the halfway house are supposed to be helping me." He exhaled long through his nose. "I don't know. Again, the thought of working is overwhelming. Even though I've been cleared, I still have to explain to a potential employer why I have nothing in my CV for eighteen years. Even when you tell someone that you were proven to be innocent, there's still that little part in the back of their mind that wonders if I'm not. If a mistake can be made once, it can be made again, right?"

Erica remained quiet. There was nothing she could say that would make anything better.

He continued, "I have my faith, and my family, and that's what I'm holding on to right now. I miss my buddies inside, though. Hell, I even miss some of the prison officers. They became like family to me, you know? The closest ones I probably will ever have, though my sisters would hate to hear me say that."

Erica offered him a sympathetic smile. "I promise I won't tell."

He shook his head. "I still can't get my head around it. The man who killed them is dead. His son now behind bars for different murders. How does someone become so twisted?"

She took a sip of her coffee. "I wish I had the answer to that."

Was it down to nature or nurture? That was a question scientists had been asking for many years now. Had these two men become what they were because of how they were raised, or did it go much deeper? Was the genetic makeup of their cells what made them killers? Studies had shown that psychopaths' brains didn't light up the same way that regular people's did. But how could a young boy growing up under those circumstances ever possibly turn out to be normal?

Liam Junior had been kept away from the rest of society by his father, not allowed any friends, and told that his mother was a bitch and a whore. The death of the mother was now also being investigated. Had she really died under natural circumstances, or had Liam's father had something to do with it? Liam had been told growing up that women were the enemy and had it drummed into him again and again, and then he had witnessed his father murdering two people in their beds. From the information they were able to get from him, he'd also been made to clean up the bloodied clothes.

When a child's brain was developing at such a rapid rate at that age, how could he possibly have grown up to be anything other than what he was? And then his father had died, though the cause was as yet unconfirmed, and Liam had somehow raised himself in that house.

That he'd been going on to live his life almost as a regular person was probably the most surprising part of all this. No one he'd worked with had had any idea that he'd be capable of such monstrosities. They'd all said he was a quiet, withdrawn man, who'd kept himself to himself.

Except for Liam, it had never been him who'd killed those people. It had always been his father.

This was something he continued to maintain.

Chapter Fifty-Three

Erica hadn't been feeling well for the past couple of weeks. She suddenly realised what day of the month it was.

Shit. She'd skipped her period.

Had she got to that stage of life already? She'd known it was close but had hoped she still had a few more years before the hot flashes started and her eyesight failed. To be fair, she hadn't actually experienced any peri-menopausal symptoms. She'd just been sick and exhausted, and her breasts—

Oh, double shit.

Not wasting another second, she raced out to the nearest pharmacy. She came home with the test smuggled in a paper bag like she was doing something illegal. Her heart thumped, and she felt hot and cold all at the same time.

Please no, please no, please no, she begged silently.

She followed the instructions, even though it wasn't the first time she'd taken one of these tests. She didn't want there to be any mistake.

She set the timer on her phone, put the test to one side, and then paced the bathroom until the timer went off.

She looked down at the pregnancy test, the word 'pregnant' appearing in the small window.

Her heart sank. The weight of the world crashed down on her shoulders. She'd never planned for this. She wasn't even sure how it had happened—not the mechanisms, of course, but the failure in the birth control. She was always so careful. She'd been adamant that she hadn't wanted another child. Poppy was the only one she needed. And it wasn't even as though she had time to take care of Poppy properly. She couldn't stand the thought of going back to those early baby days, the sleepless nights and exhaustion and the sense it was never going to end. She let the pregnancy test drop from her fingers and put her head in her hands.

"Fuck."

Exclusive offer for Erica Swift readers! Get 25% off your order using the following code at MK Farrar's direct store:
NEPHKVYNSX66
Get great deals on eBooks, audiobooks, and signed paperbacks direct from MK Farrar at mkfarrarbooks.com

. . . .

Get a free book when you sign up to M K Farrar's newsletter
mkfarrar.com

. . . .

Come and hang out with the author at MK Farrar's Crime Room – her exclusive reader's group on Facebook.

Acknowledgements

I was genuinely surprised when several of my editors and proofreaders came back to me and told me that they thought The Night Prowler was their favourite book yet. I wish I was able to condense down exactly what makes a favourite book so I could can it somehow and add it like a special sauce to all my books.

Thank you, as always, to my editor Emmy Ellis, and to my proofreaders, Jessica Fraser from Finishing by Fraser, Tammy Payne from Book Nook Nuts, and to Jacqueline Beard for always being that much needed final set of eyes.

Final thanks to you the reader, for following along with Erica and Shawn. I hope you'll keep reading!

Until next time!

MK Farrar

About the Author

••••

M K FARRAR HAS PENNED more than twenty novels of psychological noir and crime fiction. A British author, she lives in the countryside with her three children and a menagerie of rescue pets.

When she's not writing—which isn't often—she balances out all the murder with baking and binge-watching shows on Netflix.

You can find out more about M K and grab a free book via her website, https://mkfarrar.com

She can also be emailed at mk@mkfarrar.com. She loves to hear from readers!

Also by the Author

Law of Sandtown
The Scorched Girls
Under the Surface
One Final Shot

DI Erica Swift Thriller
The Eye Thief
The Silent One
The Artisan
The Child Catcher
The Body Dealer
The Mimic
The Gathering Man
The Only Witness
The Foundling

• • • •

Detective Ryan Chase Thriller
Kill Chase
Chase Down
Paper Chase
Chase the Dead

• • • •

Crime After Crime
Watching Over Me
Down to Sleep
If I Should Die

• • • •

Standalone Psychological Thrillers
Some They Lie
On His Grave
Down to Sleep

Printed in Great Britain
by Amazon